TALES FROM A RURAL ROUTE: VOLUME FIVE

TALES FROM A RURAL ROUTE: VOLUME FIVE

A HENRY COUNTY HIGH SCHOOL COLLECTION OF STUDENT MEMOIRS AND SHORT STORIES

BRINELY ADAMS SHELBY ANDERSON

RILEY DENNY JASMINE DOANE SHELBY FELKER

LOGAN MARSH NIKOLE MARTIN

JAGER MATTINGLY ADDIE MORGAN

WESLEY PERKINSON REAGAN POWELL

TAYLEE READING MILEY ROBERTS JOSHUA SHEA

PEYTON SMITH AIYANA SUTHERLAND

SARA TREECE BREANNA PERKINS

NOLAN PRATHER GEORGIA SNIDER

COLBY STIVERS KAIDEN WILSON

ISBN: 978-1-958414-37-8

Twin Sisters Press

Goshen, Kentucky 40026

twinsisterspress.com

CONTENTS

ACKNOWLEDGMENTS

A deep heartfelt thank you to author and publisher, Tony Acree, for always supporting our students and instilling in them a love for writing. - From Mrs. Burgin, the Librarian, and all of us at Henry County High School.

NO WAY OUT

BRINLEY ADAMS

Inspired by the painting “I Saw 3 Cities” by Kay Sage

I sat at my desk bored, like always, thinking about what I'm going to eat for dinner. Then my Commanding Officer, William, interrupted my thoughts, "Tomorrow at 0-900 we have a very important meeting with the higher ups, a meeting that we've wanted for a long time, be there".

Well, that cured my boredom. I listened to the briefing like I'm watching my favorite movie.

"Same way we're in the dimension we are in now... over-population is happening again, and we need another dimension to live in so we chose this newer one. They chose us to carry out the mission," William explained.

You probably don't understand, let me catch you up to speed, the year is 2378, where we are now having to take over and find new dimensions to live on because other planets aren't enough. Our technology is so advanced that we only have a handful of deaths a year making overpopulation a problem so this is our solution since we already have colonized the majority of space. Matt looks at me smiling. Matt and I have been friends for seven years now. We have had several missions together. Turns out taking over dimensions for the government together makes you grow on each other a bit. After a whole work day of talking about what the dimension and meeting is going to look like, it's finally time to go home. I don't live in a big house like other guys with lots of money, they pay extremely well when you put your life on the line for the government.

I put most of my money into my car and family, not my house. I have always been a car guy and family guy since those were special to me and my dad was a mechanic and got me into cars ever since I was 10. I live in a 2 story, 2 bathroom, and 3 bedroom house, meanwhile my car is a Lamborghini Aventador with butterfly doors. My family is spoiled because of my money. I'm not married nor do I have any kids but I am the cool uncle buying everything for my sister's kids. Time to hit the sack, I wake up, put on my uniform, go grab a coffee and off to work I go. Matt and I walk in the meeting talking about his family and how I should have a barbecue with them again sometime soon. Later follows the rest of the team that we're going on the mission with, and in walks Jessica with her long black hair, green eyes, standing tall. Josh is one of the bigger guys on the team with short dirty blonde hair. Also on the team is Katie with a ponytail in, Lucas sporting his mullet along with his trusty combat knife, and the twins, Robert and James, who are long and lanky.

"What are you guys laughing about?" Matt asked curiously.

"It's nothing, it's just what James did when he walked in the building," Katie said hysterically laughing, trying to catch her breath.

"James was walking, Lucas pantsed him and then he fell in a puddle and we all saw it," Robert said. Ignoring Robert's explanation we start the meeting. William practically shouted, "This is a dangerous mission. We have no idea what lives in this dimension and what could fight back against us so we do not split up and we do not have any funny business. Our lives will be on the line. Does everyone understand?"

"YES SIR," we all yell.

"We roll out in 15 minutes, get your gear and get ready." William said. Everyone grabs their stuff for their job in the mission. William is leader, Josh is second in command, Katie is Comms, Matt is Demolition, I'm Scout, Jessica is Group Lead, James is Operational Specialist, Robert is the other Scout, and Lucas is Lookout. "Time to go." Josh said.

The city we land in is dead silent with no one in sight. "Great start," I said.

"Why do we have weapons if there's nothing to use them on?" James questioned.

"You'll see." William replied. The city landscape was something I had never seen before. There were tall, weirdly shaped buildings, with uneven spacing and each building apart from each other. There was no geological features either. No hills, mountains, just flat. The air had no scent. All the buildings had no color. Everything was just gray and white. I could see that everyone is unsettled by the place we landed in. But we had a mission to complete so we pressed forward. We found a town with multiple colorless shops, a police station, and a central courthouse.

"It's getting late, we should find somewhere to make camp," Jessica noted.

"We'll make camp in that courthouse, in the center where we can see if anyone is sneaking up on us," William insisted.

Inside it was large and just like outside, there was no color. I am starting to regret coming along on the mission. I should have called in sick. Matt sets up his gear and starts helping with mine.

"I feel like something is off." Matt says to me.

"You're not the only one feeling that way, trust me." I replied.

"I'm feeling like this mission is going to be different... end different" I commented.

"Copy and paste brother... copy and paste." Matt replied.

It was strange that Matt felt that way. He isn't scared of anything. One time we went on a fishing trip and he caught a shark but we couldn't get it on the boat. I jokingly told him to get in the water and bring it up. He did exactly that because he fears nothing. After that I gave him the nickname "Superman." I sat my gear next to Matt and Katie. Before I dozed off into sleep I saw Lucas staring at his watch.

I was sleeping when I heard an eerie noise.

"Wha-" Matt's sleep was also interrupted by the same noise. We hear an echo loud enough that the whole team wakes up. We are all waiting for it to happen again.

"Where's Lucas and William?" Josh asked.

"That's a good question," James responded.

We wait for another echo but instead we get a scream. William's scream.

"FALL OUT!" Josh commanded.

We all grab our weapons and run. Everyone ran to different parts of the courthouse. Matt and I are together hiding behind a desk. We heard more screams from William. He was yelling for help. Matt and I run over towards the screams but James stops us. Putting his finger to his lips we look at what is around the corner. The thing that attacked us is now holding William by the head lifeless. The monster is tall, muscular and doesn't have any skin, just muscle and bone. It threw Williams' now dead body across the room. Matt snuck his way around the beast hinting for us to surround him or create a distraction. James and I then snuck around the front of the room. James threw one of his 9mm magazines in the corner. The monster heard it and ran towards it. We then see Matt silently make use of his demolition kit, setting a bomb where it once stood. He then threw his 9mm mag right where the bomb was and the creature ran right towards the noise. When the creature gets close enough to the bomb we all covered our ears.

BOOM. The rest of the team came running in from the noise.

"What was that?" Jessica asked.

"Me killing what attacked us" Matt replied.

"Good job Matt, where is William?" Robert asked.

"Dead," James replied.

"What do you mean dead?" Jessica asked. I point to where William lies on the ground completely still, all twisted up, and bloody.

"What about Lucas?" James asked.

"Scared and covered in blood from his near encounter with death," I explained.

"Okay, at least we didn't lose two people," James said, relieved.

We started heading back and there waiting for us was Lucas. He looked scared to death and halfway cleaned up. We headed back to William grabbing his helmet and rifle, placing the helmet on top of the rifle. With the rifle standing up we told Command that our lead was KIA, that although it was still night here we will try to progress with little sleep. Soon after, we looked out the window and there were thousands of the creatures waiting outside the courthouse door... waiting for us to come out.

"Seems like they heard the big bang." Jessica said.

"So we're stuck here... great, just great." Lucas said

"What are we going to do?" asked Jessica.

"We can't just sit in here and wait. We need to find a way out of here," Lucas said.

"We set a trap and make our final stand," Josh said

Lucas snapped, "With all due respect we aren't going to be able to fight all of those off an-"

"Did you not hear the part where I said final stand, we don't just get out of here easy, we're as good as dead." Josh interrupted. But then we heard church bells and we looked out the window and all of them were in awe as they heard it and started heading back to wherever they came from. Lucas was already at the door telling us to hurry up and we all ran down towards him entering the street again. We saw one of them glance back at us and stare for a while but then continued on with the rest. We all stood there confused and wondering what miracle just happened.

"Soooo, what just happened?" I asked.

"That's a good question," Matt added.

"I don't know but I am not gonna complain, let's keep moving, we have a job to do." Josh said.

We were back on foot exploring the rest of the town when I saw a giant central tower in the middle of a field surrounded by random shapes.

"Do we go in over there?" I asked pointing to the building

"That doesn't seem suspicious at all," James said.

"We'll check it out later," Josh whispered. We continued to look at what was around us as the sun began to rise. Maybe the creatures only came out at certain times of day like some kind of sci-fi monster or a vampire since we only saw them at night. We decided to explore the countryside of the dimension now. Then all of the sudden everything went black, just black. One second it was morning and now all of the sudden it was night. Like someone flipped a light switch. We all stayed quiet just in case something was in the darkness that we couldn't see. It's part of our training to stay low and not be heard or spotted when stuff like this happens. The training for that was an absolute blast though; it was like blind hide and seek. I was a seeker one time and I ended up chasing one of my own teammates through the dark in circles trying to catch them. I tried to remember this training as I sat in absolute fear waiting for something to just grab me and it be over within a blink of an eye.

We all waited and waited until a familiar voice was heard in the darkness. It was William telling us it's okay and to come in his direction. We all heard it because we all started looking in that way, I see fear in everyone's eyes except Matt, seems like he's starting to be fearless again. We all slowly inched toward what sounded like William, expecting something else to be there but it's William standing up completely fine like last night never happened.

"William?" Lucas asked.

We all are still being completely silent, not sure what to do. Lucas broke out of our secure formation walking toward William.

"Lucas, get back here." James and Katie both whispered.

But Lucas kept going. He got right next to what must be a

fake William and proceeds to hug it as if they were long lost friends.

"I thought you were dead, I thought I was a goner but you saved me, I'm so sorry I couldn't help," Lucas goes on.

We all lowered our weapons because whatever it was that looked like William, seemed friendly. However, when I saw something glimmer through fake William's chest I began to aim my gun at him.

"What are you doing? It's okay, nothing is happening." James explained.

Still aiming at William I pointed to the shining thing peeking through his chest, James must have seen it because he too started raising his weapon at him.

"LUCAS GET BACK!" Robert yelled.

But it's too late. There is a giant metal spear going through his heart that basically leapt out of William. James and I started firing to neutralize the target. Matt ran up to Lucas pulling him away, but we realize we've got company. We heard a lot of roars. We all got in a secure formation pointing our weapons in multiple different directions. Katie threw a flare into the darkness to see what was out there and we saw a mob of four-legged creatures with sharp teeth mouth wide open ready to attack and we all opened fire on what surrounded us. We were all watching every direction, still in formation.

"WE'RE GONNA RUN OUT OF AMMO SOON!" Jessica yelled over the gunfire.

"WE'VE GOTTA MAKE A RUN FOR IT!" Matt yelled.

"ON 3 WE RUN," Josh yells "3...2...1, GO!"

And we all started running towards a tower. I heard them right behind me as I started firing behind us to keep them off us.

"I SEE THE TOWER!" Robert yelled.

"HELP!" I yelled as I felt something grab my leg and put me onto the ground. I fought it the best I could but to no avail. It grabbed my arms so I couldn't do anything. This is it, I'm done. But then I heard someone behind me hitting the creature with a hammer. It's a masked man that helps me up and points towards the tower to run, so I do. Behind me I heard him taking out the monsters behind me but soon his scream joined the thousand others I heard in the dark. I made it to the tower in time to close it with Matt covering me as I ran in. Inside was my group and a city worth of people inside staring at us. Speaking perfect English, one asked,"Who are you guys?"

"The Marine Corp of Dimension 653334," Josh said.

"You shouldn't have come here," another voice replied.

"What is happening here?" I asked.

"The creatures of the night came to get you, because you killed one of them," another told us.

We spend the next two hours trying to figure out who these people are and what those things are outside. They explained the creatures outside only live in the darkness and if you kill one you basically have a bounty on your head for murdering one of them. They told us that they send squads outside each morning to get supplies and the ones who do come back tell everyone else who they lost. They also use the people they previously killed to trick the ones they know. We saw that first hand with William, the time of day is also random. One day will be 24 hours and the next day it could be 10 minutes. They said that once you're here there is no way out. They also told us that they all were from the Marine Corps as well that all requested to be rescued out of the dimension but the rescue squad never came. Because allegedly there are only ways in and no ways out. They also warn that we will be killed if we try to leave. They said that the other Marines have already been killed and that we will not be the exception. They also gave us a list of rules that we must follow if we want to stay with them.

We headed out in the morning to find supplies for them to make us earn our worth staying. I paired up with Matt to go help a group of people find medical supplies since they're down low. We made our way down, and upon arriving at the hospital in the city. We found a group of survivors waiting for us to come help them, but it will be night soon so we decided to stay in the hospital. While waiting for night to pass. I looked out and I could hear the screams of the unfortunate lives down there. We heard a knock and pleas at the door. It was Josh begging to be let in. I rushed to the door to help but one of the other people stopped me.

"You let him in, they'll know where we are, they've wounded him and can track, don't open that door," they told me.

"NO, NO, NOOOOO," I heard Josh yell.

A creature then sideswiped him and there was nothing left of him. Just his blood and his upper half, which was later taken by another creature. I stared out into the darkness hoping all of this was just a dream. But regardless of me pinching and punching myself nothing changed except more bruises on my body.

The next morning we headed back to the camp where we met up with the other people and only Jessica and Robert. No Katie or James in sight. Nine of us went in and there's only four left within the span of 3 days.

We spent a few weeks helping these people and kind of started getting used to it. We were trying to find Katie's communication equipment to contact. Since they wouldn't come for rescues we'll tell them we finished the mission and hope that peaks their interest in coming to get us and the others. Since we were going out each night together a few times we asked Robert where Katie was taken and he said the deeper part in the city that was pretty far away. One hundred twenty-five miles to be exact, so we were now on the hunt for a military box that could have been destroyed in the attack but we watched each other's backs pretty well. We brought a few others with us to help retrieve the equipment, but just like other missions we were dropping like flies each day. Especially since it can literally just turn pitch black anytime it wants to. We were holding out in a church still needing 52 miles to get there. It was going to be a long road but with the random time changes it could take us forever to get there.

"50 miles to go guys," Robert said.

"As long as we don't run into any trouble, which is impossible here," Matt interjected.

"Just be on your toes and watch the sky to make sure there aren't any hints of it turning dark," I said. We go on for another 20 or so miles when it turns pitch black.

"Not this again," Jessica said.

"Do you see any buildings?" I asked.

"Last building I saw was 15 miles East," Matt said.

"Then we stay here in an open field for the rest of the night and hope we live," one of the others said. We saw movement in the bushes. As we started aiming our weapons ready to fire, out came James. We had seen this before. We all were about to shoot when one of the creatures tries to pounce on James but he dodged out of the way just in time. That's when I realized it's the real James. He must have lived alone somewhere for a while.

"James?" Jessica says confused.

"Hi!" James said, sounding weak.

"We thought you were dead," I explained.

"Well, when you have skills like me you survive the impossible. I've survived being in the open ever since I got Katie's equipment. I was trying to find you guys."

Now that James has the equipment we might get out of here alive. He started running and we followed him while Matt and Robert covered us. James tried to pry open a jammed metal door. When we noticed his struggle, Jessica and I started helping him.

"Any day now guys!" Matt said.

"I'm running low, please hurry!" Robert said anxiously.

We opened the door just in time as Robert got hit in the leg, and we all rushed in. Matt and Robert were nowhere to be seen. We looked out the window and Matt was trying to carry Robert inside. I opened the door and started to cover them, but then I remembered that once you're wounded they know where you are at all times, like one of the others said with Josh. I quickly grabbed Matt and pulled him in with Robert. It was not over though. We had to send Robert out otherwise we would be attacked all night and soon they'd get in.

"I'm sorry sir but you're a dead man," one of the others said to Robert.

"And you'll kill us all if you don't leave," James added.

"No, No, I'm fine. We can fight them, we'll be fine," Robert replied.

"Well, too bad, you're not going to stay here," someone said while pointing a gun at him.

"Just like that you're just gonna kill me because I got a scratch?" Robert asked.

"No, I'm going to kill you because it's either you or all of us," the man with the gun replied.

"But I have a family, a little girl, you can't do this to me." Robert pleaded desperately.

"We've all got families," the others said.

Robert went for his gun but was shot by one of the others before he could do anything. They tossed his body outside to be taken by the creatures. The beating on the roof stopped and we now all waited for something to happen just in case someone mentions what just happened with Robert. After a few minutes of silence we started to talk again.

"James, do you have the radio?" I asked.

"Yes, why?" James questioned.

"We're gonna call Base and tell them we need to be brought back home because we completed the mission," I explained.

"But we didn't." James said.

"I know but they won't come if we ask for a rescue apparently."

“That puts our dimension in danger because they'll be able to jump through!" James claimed.

We think about it before we all agree that we need to call them to get everyone out of here safely. While James made the call of “mission complete” we talked about how we were going to get there. Then we heard a smash and a gunshot. We ran in to see what happened. James had smashed the radio and killed himself. Now we are stuck in this dimension forever waiting for the next group to come by wishing it is soon but until then we are here, and there is no escape. Dejected, we went back to the camp, bringing them the bad news and telling them that we are now waiting for the next group of people to come. We are waiting for a miracle to happen. We are hopeless. We are all hopeless. Secretly wishing someone will come and help us. But until then, we are trapped in this dimension, with no way out.

SENSATIONAL NEWS

SHELBY ANDERSON

Here is the story of my walk to fame. It all started with a call.

"Will you be willing to help out with the annual Halloween play this year?"

"Yes, of course!" I shouted over the phone. I pity the person on the receiving end for having an atomic blast of pure joy and excitement right into their ear. Although I feel sorry for yelling, one cannot contain their enthusiasm when one can see their dream becoming reality.

Walking into the theater for my first day of rehearsal, I was welcomed by a colossal mountain of Halloween decor. The decorations filled the entrance of the local theater and spilled out onto the rest of the building. We have close to 1000 pumpkins, 400 witches, 70 black cats, and 20 zombies. The theater receives donations of Halloween decorations, but this may just be an opportunity for people to get rid of their broken Halloween decorations.

I stand there admiring the immense pile when the stage manager taps me on the shoulder.

"You ready to sort?" he said to me with a sweet smile.

Ummm... excuse me? Sort!? I thought. Here I thought I was going to have the time of my life directing, acting, or even something of importance, but no. I was called on to sort a pile of cheap, broken, old Halloween decorations. I hid my disappointment because it was still a great opportunity and began making piles. One for pumpkins, one for bats, another for trash, and 12 other sections. The mountain slowly shrank.

Amidst my sorting, I found a beautiful, intricately designed oak wood box. This had been the first thing that didn't look like it came from a Dollar Tree twenty years ago. With my interest peaked, I wiped the dust off and began to open the lock. The box was lined with soft, red velvet fabric. At the bottom, there was a pile of small brown sticks. I examined the material closer. I found that these were bones.

The bones looked old and like they once belonged to a bird. A large bird. Maybe a raven, a toucan, or a parrot. I'm no ornithologist. I don't know what to do with these. I bring the box of bones to the lead director.

"Take a look at these,"

"Wow! This is gorgeous! It certainly sticks out compared to the rest of the decor," he exclaimed.

"I know, what should I do with them?" I ask as the director looks at me with a sort of mischievous look.

"How would you feel about putting these bones back together?"

"That sounds great!"

It actually doesn't. What am I supposed to do with this? Although it may be hard, it will be more fun than sorting the rest of the decorations. I also didn't want to disappoint. Maybe if they see I work well, I could get a more important role. With this, I took a seat on the stage because it happened to be the only clear spot in the theater. I slowly began reconstructing the bird.

With the help of a textbook diagram (which also happened to be a donation) and a tube of superglue, the ribcage started to come together. With my lack of understanding of bird anatomy and the glue causing my fingers to stick to the bones, my clothes, and each other, this task was rather difficult, but I continued the puzzle. After what seemed like an eternity, the bones began to take shape into something more. The skeleton no longer seemed complex. It became second nature. The bones naturally found their way to each other and stayed together in perfect harmony.

The longer I looked at the bird, the stronger the hold it had on me. The breathtaking beauty of the bones that had once soared through the air now soars through my mind. The bones slowly crept back into the shape of the bird.

Then something unexpected happened, the skeleton grew, developing muscles, organs, and blood. The bird was then covered in a blanket of skin. Feathers in colors of red, blue, and yellow popped up and covered the rest of the body. The bird was alive.

The bird took flight. My mind told me it was vital to follow this bird. I go to stand but my feet struggle to move. I look down and my legs are tangled in a mess of vines. I twist and twirl to free myself. To prevent this from happening once more, I leap to find the bird.

I find the bird climbing higher. I think to myself I must find the answers to this bird. Why did it come to life? Why would someone just give away this?

I climbed up a tree. I come closer to the bird yet the bird is still distant. The bird reached above the tree line. Extending my arm to capture the bird, I could not reach it. Feeling the warmth of the sun on my cheek I notice I am transcending the tree. The bird flies into the sun and takes me with it. My skin grew hotter. My eyes turned brighter until the world went black. Darkness and nothing covered the yellow light and the colorful little bird.

I awake in a cold, white room.

"Where am I?" I ask the only other person with me in the room.

"She's awake!" The person leaves the room and the number of people surrounding me that I don't know triples, then I see my family. My family surrounds me. They look relieved, but I have no idea why.

"What's going on?" I raise my voice demanding an answer.

"You were in a coma, honey. You even made it on the

front page of the newspaper. You're kind of a celebrity." My mother finally explained to me.

"I'm in the newspaper for being in a coma?" The confusion is still overwhelming.

"Here, read this." My sister passed me a rolled-up newspaper.

Sensational News!

A local student falls into a coma during a rehearsal of an annual Halloween play.

Florence David was a member of the team for the annual Halloween play. While sorting donated decorations she spontaneously bursts into interpretive dance. Her performance caught the attention of fellow cast members. The head director explains the event from his perspective.

"I went to find Florence to see how far along her construction of a prop had been. When I got to her she was on the stage. The floor belonged to her. It was as if she was possessed by an unseen force. I went to find my peers to show them this astonishing performance. I regretted my decision to make her a stagehand. She should've been the lead!-"

I paused my reading.

"I don't understand. I wasn't even in the theater. I wasn't performing. It must have been someone else." My mother who often talked like this said, "I know sometimes performers say they are possessed by another being while they perform. Is that what you mean?"

"No, I mean it couldn't have been me. I got lost somewhere in the forest and there was the bird who came to life and I followed it to the sun, then the world went blank." My mom, clearly still bewildered by my explanation, told me to keep reading the article.

"The performance moved up the stage. She took a risk and climbed to the top toward the stage light. I have never seen a talent like that presented on this stage before. It was sensational! My amazement quickly turned to horror as she plummeted to the floor. As she was unresponsive, we called 911.-"

I know that I was quite literally in a coma, but I know what I saw.

"Did you find the bird?" I asked to hopefully find an answer.

"There was a pile of broken bird bones and a box under you when the ambulance arrived. Is that what you are talking about?" my father replied.

"Yes, what happened to them?"

"They were thrown away, there was no reason to keep them because of the damage."

It is no use. I can hardly believe what happened. Maybe it didn't happen. Maybe it was all a delusion. Maybe I didn't drink enough water that day, or maybe being surrounded by dust and plastic can change the way the mind works.

Later that week, I was visited by the head director of the play. After a lot of small talk, he got to the real reason why he was there. He asked me if I was willing to be a bigger part of the play next year after I recovered. Although I experienced the most traumatic event of my life in that theater, it is still my dream to be on the stage.

A year later the play came around again. No coma, no weird delusions, but a hire from New York City. I hope you can guess where this leads.

The man saw me in the play as the lead. Pulled the head director aside and asked if he could speak to me. He did and here I am. Telling the story of the greatest, yet most terrifying moments of my life.

SEALED WITH A KISS

RILEY DENNY

Inspired by the painting "The Kiss" by Francesco Hayez

He finally did it, I should've seen it coming. It feels right. I just passed by, he grabbed my wrist and pulled me in. I can feel the chills go down my spine. Not only that, but I want to fall into him, but I don't know if I can. We are in the middle of all these people, someone will surely tell my dad. My father, the king, Augustus Wingate, is a powerful-looking man with gray hair and a short beard. Then there is me, Delilah Wingate. I am named after my mother, who passed away when I was only three years old. Throughout my entire life, I have wondered what my life would be like if I had a mother to look up to. I wonder what my father would have been like had my mother still been alive.

I am a teen girl who has lived in these dark, empty halls of the castle for her whole life. Playing games with my only "friends": my lady-in-waiting, butler, and court guards. These are all people my dad insists I have. Since I was young, we have played games, many of which consist of me running around, my blonde hair hitting me in the face, while they chased me. Or sitting and playing a board game. But now I am eighteen, there is not much playing. I just sit in my big room on a bed that feels less comforting than usual. The rain hitting the window making it hard to learn how to become the "perfect" queen and wife I should be.

Ronan Ellington, though, is a nineteen-year-old boy. He is not well known and is not part of any royal status. But, he is the guy I found myself attracted to, and he is the guy with whom I sealed my love story with a kiss.

Let's rewind.

Spring in Rosenden, the grass is green, and the flowers are all in bloom. When I rarely go out into the town for my dress fittings, I can see the bright, blue sky from almost anywhere. But, the week before, it was all rain and no sun.

That day was the first day it was sunny, with clear skies. The trees and grass were greener than I had ever seen, and the flowers had bloomed with bright, vibrant colors. Since it had been so dreary last week, I thought I might go for a walk that day.

"Father," I asked in the darkness of his office, "would it be possible for me to walk through the town?"

"Sure," he answered, "but, you will need to take a court guard with you."

He didn't even have to say it. I knew he would make me take someone with me. He has always made someone go with me whenever I go into town. It was annoying when it started. I was 14, and I was allowed to go into town "by myself." Little did I know, this meant I would have someone with me at all times, for the rest of my life.

I finally got out of the palace with my court guard. I had on a blue dress, and my hair was around my shoulders. The fresh air felt cool on my skin, and the sun was sinking into my skin and warming my body. As I walk through the town, I catch glimpses of people looking and staring at me.

"Though it is rare for me to go out, I don't feel as though it should be weird for other people I do," I thought to myself.

Today there was a farmers market going on, so there were many people all around. I went to look at some flowers that were being sold at a small, wooden stand with flowers bordering it. But most importantly, I noticed the man working at the stand. He seemed to be young—my age, he was tall and slim, and his hair was a deep brown color. During this time, I seemed to have lost my court guard, so I decided not to go any further. Instead, I strolled over to the flower stand.

As I went up to the flower stand, I was a little nervous. I never interacted with people my age, at least not as a teenager, and I am not one to go up to someone I think is cute. This was a different and new experience for me.

When I went up to him, it was a normal customer-service interaction. I expected him to treat me a little differently since I am a part of the royal family. But he didn't. In his eyes, I was just like everyone else, he didn't even know my name. It was freeing in a way, the fact I could just be here without the pressure of being a princess. At that moment, I realized he wasn't someone my dad would be okay with me being in a relationship with.

"But what if I just got to know him?" I thought.

I walked away thinking about the interaction I just had with him. I went to find my court guard when I felt someone touch my shoulder. I turned around to find it was the flower stand boy.

"You forgot your flowers," he breathlessly said to me. It was as if he had been running after me.

"Oh, thank you so much," I responded. "I can be so clueless sometimes."

"You're welcome," he said with a smirk.

I didn't know what to do or how to feel at that moment, all I knew was my father would not have approved of the feelings I was having. This made it hard for me to decide what I would do next. But, I decided I would not lose my one chance at finding true love.

"Hey, would you like to show me around the town? I haven't seen much of it," I asked him as we stood in the middle of the street.

He responded, "Um, I guess, I just need to get someone to cover the stand first."

"Ok, I will come with you then," I said, a little too eagerly.

We went over to the flower stand, and as we did, there wasn't much said. But, I knew, or at least hoped, we would talk more as the day went on. He found someone to cover the stand, and we were on our way. That was when I realized we hadn't even introduced ourselves yet.

"I am so sorry, I haven't introduced myself..." I started.

"I know who you are, Delilah Wingate," he said.

"Wait, you do?" I questioned, "Well, if you know me, then why don't I know your name?"

This all felt a little uncomfortable, but at the same time, it felt smooth and right.

"I'm Ronan Ellington." He laughed.

"Ronan," I thought, "is an interesting name, but it fits him."

"Well, Ronan, should we start on my tour?" I asked.

"Sure, but why do you need a tour? You are the princess, aren't you?" He replied.

That made me think—sure, I was the princess, I had that title, but I didn't even know my town. I felt a little caught off guard by his question, but I understood where it was coming from.

As we started walking through the town, we also started talking about everything. We talked about our families, our dreams, and our futures. Mine is not very interesting, I have to continue the royal family tree, it is up to me and only me to continue it. But, Ronan has actual dreams and aspirations, which include traveling, starting a family, and running his own business. I realized we had different paths, but I didn't want that to get in the way of what we might become.

For the next couple of weeks, we hung out and talked regularly. I was falling in love with him, and he was with me. Of course, we did all of this without my dad knowing. If he found out, he would be so furious with me.

Ronan and I were in the middle of the street on a busy day in town, we couldn't keep doing this. We are in the middle of all these people, someone will surely tell my dad. So we had to say goodbye, at least for now.

There were so many emotions going through my mind. We said goodbye. I was walking away in the middle of the street, where we had first met.

OBSESSED

JAZMIN DOANE

Inspired by the painting "The Lovers" by Rene Margritte

As I walked down the loud chaotic sidewalks of New York City I was too focused on the huge billboards to realize the man in front of me until my coffee that was once in my hand was now all over my clothes. I was so mad and shocked because all my life nobody has ever bumped into me causing me to spill my coffee all over myself. I heard the man apologizing and as I looked up at him he pulled out a bright red cloth from his jacket pocket and handed it to me to wipe my face and neck off. He was a very tall dark man wearing a black suit, with dark green eyes and jet black hair. He caught my attention back when he took off his jacket revealing his muscular arms under his white long sleeve turtleneck he had on underneath his jacket and wrapped the jacket around my shoulders. He told me he was extremely sorry and offered to buy me a coffee, and of course I agreed because who would I be to decline a coffee from a handsome stranger who just made my last coffee my whole wardrobe? We walked to a café down the street. When we got in, it was so warm I forgot I had been freezing from the coffee on my clothes and because it does get pretty cold in New York in November. We found a table for two and sat. He ordered an americano coffee and I ordered a pumpkin spice latte.

"I'm honestly not surprised by your drink of choice," I told him.

"And why is that?" he asked with a smile.

"I don't know, you just seem like the type," I said as I blushed from his bright smile.

"Well, my name is Miguel, and you?"

"Elaine but you can call me Elly, everyone does," I said as I looked into his beautiful big green eyes.

"Elaine. I like that name," he said sweetly.

I was a bit aggravated because I didn't really like my real name and nobody called me it except my mother when she got angry at me but I let it go because I could just tell he wasn't going to call me Elly. It felt like we talked for hours but yet I still knew nothing about him, eventually I thanked him for my coffee and went on my way. I got back to my house and started getting ready to take a shower when I realized I still had on Miguel's jacket. I knew I had to get it back to him but I don't know how because I have no way of contacting him.

I got out of the shower and hung Miguel's jacket up in my closet and laid in bed with my dog, Drako, until I fell asleep. The next morning I woke up and made myself breakfast and got ready to take my dog for a walk. As I was getting ready to walk out the door I got a follow request on Instagram by *@Miguel264_*. How did he find my Instagram? My username isn't even really my name so I was confused on how he would've looked me up and found me. I usually only accept family and friends but I knew this was him so I accepted his request and messaged him,

"How did you find my instagram?"

Now I was too concerned about how he found my Instagram and forgot all about taking Drako for a walk. I was in the kitchen waiting for his reply when after moments of pacing for what felt like forever he wrote me back and simply said, "You were on my suggested friends."

"Yeah right. We just met last night and I'm already popping up on your suggested friends the next morning? Unbelievable." I texted.

"Okay, don't believe me but I´m telling the truth," he responded.

I hooked Drako to his leash and headed out the door. We walked for a good 30 minutes and even went to the dog park which we don't usually do when it's cold out.

After we got back from our walk I got Drako some food and sat down in the living room to start on my school work for nursing school when my phone vibrated. I didn't even have to look at my phone because I already knew it was him. I picked up my phone and read, “You still have my jacket.”

I replied, "Yes, do you want it back?”

“Yes, I do, meet me at the café?” he asked.

“Maybe around 3, I’m doing my school work right now... now please stop texting me.”

“Okay, see you at 3.” he responded with a smiley face.

I put my phone on *Do Not Disturb* and tried to focus back on my work but I couldn’t. Meeting up with him was stuck in my mind so I put my laptop down and turned on the TV. I watched some shows slowly falling asleep. I woke up around 1:30, took a shower, and got ready. I wanted to try to present myself well in front of Miguel.

When 2:40 came I left my house and started walking to the café. I have a car but I prefer to walk if I’m not going far and fall is my favorite season so I enjoyed walking in the weather. When I got there I saw Miguel sitting in the back corner at a table. He was wearing gray sweatpants with a black long sleeve shirt and a vest on. I joined him at the table and handed him his jacket. We got coffee and of course he still got an americano. We talked for a while. I told him I was in nursing school to be a RN and he told me he was an entrepreneur. I knew when I first saw him that he had money but now he just proved my point right but he didn't brag or mention money and I loved that.

He offered to walk me home and I accepted his offer, a few minutes later we left and headed for my house. When we got there I asked him if he wanted to come in and he did, I introduced him to Drako and around my apartment but Drako started growling at him so I locked him in my room so Miguel wouldn't be frightened. My apartment is small but I keep it clean and organized,

"Messy is too chaotic and overwhelms me," I told him.

He laughed and told me it was a good thing that I kept my apartment clean. We sat in the kitchen and I made us smoothies. Smoothies and working out were really my thing because I really got into them after my mother passed away. I told him about how I have not stopped going to the gym and eating healthy since. As we talked some more it felt like I knew him better but I could still tell there was something he wasn't telling me. He went with me to walk Drako before he left since it was getting late and now dark outside but he kept his distance from Drako. Drako was still acting weird toward Miguel and didn't like it when he got close to me and I didn't understand why. When we got back to my apartment I told him I enjoyed his company and it was nice seeing him again. He thanked me for giving him his jacket back. I got ready for bed after he left and went to sleep because I had to be up early in the morning for work.

That night I jumped awake in a puddle of my own sweat. I had a nightmare about Miguel. He had me locked in a big clear box with only a bed in what looked like a basement. He would only come down to give me food and water every few hours. The other times he came down I would wake up chained to a chair and he would start to cut little pieces of skin off my body.

As he did I woke up from the nightmare. I got up and got some water to try to calm myself down and eventually went back to sleep. I didn't have any more nightmares that night and woke up in the morning to get ready for work. I had to be up at 4:30am so I could be at work by six. I work at a nursing home trying to further my career in nursing until I get my degree. When I got in my car about to leave for work my phone vibrated... it was Miguel. I really didn't want anything to do with him after my nightmare last night because I believe that dreams are a sign and I didn't know what he could possibly want now that he got his jacket back. The message said,"Are you busy today?"

I didn't open his message and left for work. I didn't have time to text him.

Later that day when I took my lunch break I noticed that I had three new messages from Miguel. I didn't know he had texted me because I keep my phone on *Do Not Disturb* while I'm at work so I don't get distracted. He said, "Hello?" followed by, "Are you gonna text me back?" And the last message said, "Fine, I'll see you after you get off work."

I was anxious because how did he know I was at work? How did he even know I had a job? I never told him anything about having a job and why is he blowing my phone up? He is acting crazy and obsessed with me and we've only hung out twice. I am officially done with him. I blocked him on Instagram and tried to find something else to do to keep my mind off it but all I could think about it is how he knows where I live.

WHY WOULD I LET HIM IN MY APARTMENT? My mind was racing. I was stressed and nervous, completely overwhelmed with so many thoughts and emotions I started to panic. My co-worker, Alysia, came over and helped me calm down and I told her what was happening. We were working the same shift so she offered to follow me home when we got off work to make me feel better. I told her yes and thanked her greatly. When I got off my break I was focused back on work but still had the thoughts in the back of my mind.

Eventually, it was two in the afternoon and I was off work. I waited for Alyssia by the door. She got to the door and went out of the building and we got into our cars. I looked in my mirror to make sure she was following me. When we arrived at my apartment I saw Miguel standing at the doorway to my apartment building holding a pumpkin spice latte. Alyssia walked up with me and Miguel told me he just wanted to talk.

"Please just leave me alone," I muttered while walking past him into the building. I asked Alyssia if she could stay for a bit and she agreed that it would be safer. When I got up to my apartment I knew I had to walk Drako but I didn't want to go back out there around Miguel,

"Shit, what am I gonna do about Drako? He has to go outside," I told Alyssia.

"I will walk him for you Elly," she offered.

"NO! You can't go out there by that crazy maniac by yourself. What if he's still here? What if he tries to kidnap you? I'm going with you!" I insisted.

"Okay we can walk him together and if he tries to do anything weird we will run to the pizza place across the street and call the police," Alyssia said.

We walked out of the building and Miguel was not standing by the door anymore but I saw him sitting in a car staring at us. We walked Drako down the street and back. Fortunately we did not have to run to the pizza place and call the police. We made it safely back inside. Alyssia and I sat down in the living room and I told her all about Miguel and how we met. She suggested that if Miguel bothers me or messages me anymore to report him to the police. She ended up leaving around eight and I took a shower and got ready for bed. I don't remember falling asleep but again I woke up in the middle of the night soaked in my own sweat. I had the same nightmare but this time it was longer. The nightmare continued with him cutting small pieces of my skin off throughout the day until I woke up. I got a glass of water, turned a show on the TV and drifted back off to sleep, when I woke up the next morning I wasn't in my bed I was in the clear box from my nightmares, I thought I was dreaming again until Miguel came down the stairs and said, "Hello Elaine."

"HOW DID YOU GET ME DOWN HERE? WHAT IS WRONG WITH YOU? ARE YOU INSANE?!" I screamed at him with tears coming down my face. He ignored me, put a plate of eggs on a tray and then into the box. Afterward he immediately walked back upstairs. When he was gone I checked everywhere for my phone but it wasn't with me. He must have taken it. I wasn't in my original clothes that I went to sleep in. I was in a pink matching pajama set. I had nothing in this box but a twin sized bed and a plate of eggs. I have to find a way to get out of here before he started doing what he did in my nightmare... *But how?* Miguel came back down the stairs.

"Why haven't you eaten any of your eggs?" he asked.

"I'm not hungry," I murmured.

"Well, you need to eat! At least a little bit so you aren't hungry," he said.

I picked up the plate and ate the eggs with my hands while Miguel stared at me creepily. I sat back on the bed and started to feel dizzy, the next thing I knew I was out cold. When I woke up I was chained to a chair just like I had been in my nightmares except Miguel was sitting across from me holding a knife. He looked like he had been waiting for me to wake up.

"How are you feeling?" he asked me.

I ignored him. He must have put something in the eggs to make me pass out so that he could get me out of the box and chain me to this chair. My worst fear came true and he took the knife to my skin and started to cut. I screamed in agonizing pain when he was done. But I had a plan. He was sitting so close to me that I slammed my head into his head as hard as I possibly could. He fell out of his chair and held his head. My vision started to get blurry from hitting his head so hard but I focused on getting out of this chair and escaping this insane man.

I rocked in the chair back and forth but it didn't help. It hurt but I squeezed my hands out of the chairs. Miguel had passed out from hitting his head on the hard concrete floor so I scooted my chair to him and started going through all his pockets trying to find the keys to unchain my feet. Eventually I found them in his left pants pocket and unlocked the key to the chain. As I did he woke up and tried to grab me. We fell on the floor fighting and he had his hand wrapped around my mouth so I couldn't scream but I bit his hand as hard as I could. He screamed in pain from my bite and I grabbed the knife off the floor and stabbed him in his chest. I ran up the stairs but there was a lock on the door. I had to go back down and get the keys.

With the knife still in my hand I ran down the stairs and grabbed the keys that laid next to his body, as I did he tried grabbing my hand and I stabbed him in the neck. FINALLY, he was dead, I didn't have to worry about him anymore. *My life was back to normal, thanks to my dreams.*

CAMP MURDERER

SHELBY FELKER

Inspired by the painting "The Gleaners" by Jean-Francois Millet

On a quiet, foggy, cool summer morning everything was still as the sun rose above the tree line in the hay field. The birds chirping made it a peaceful morning until the scream of a young child woke the two camp owners from the restful sleep. The two men ran out of their cabins and towards that same tree line the sun had been touching in the very back of the hay field. Steam grew as they got closer. They continued to run while the chill wind blew in their faces. They slowed their run to a jog as they found themselves a little lost because they heard the scream from all different directions. They walked in one direction of where the steam seemed to be coming from. Suddenly, it stopped. No screams were heard, but they did hear a stick break to their left. When the two men turned they found something extremely shocking. A girl, young, maybe eight or nine years old. She hung there by her ankles and was gutted like a deer. One of the men got sick at the sight of the way she looked. The other stood in shock. He walked slowly to her, took the knife out from his back pocket and cut the rope that was holding her up. There was something he saw on the tree, something...familiar.

"Hey Moore, doesn't this look like the symbol we used for that ghost story we told the campers last year?" one man asked the other while pointing at the symbol on the tree.

Moore replied, still retching, "Uh, yeah it does, why?"

"Oh, I don't know. Maybe because it's drawn in blood!" Barker exclaimed. "And it looks like it was hers," he continued while pointing at the girl lying on the ground. They both started walking back to the camp and discussed what they're going to do about her.

"We can't leave her there. The campers are supposed to go on a hike today. She can't stay there." Barker said to Moore as they walked on the smoothed dirt path back to the field. After they locked the gate and turned around to face the campers' cabins they saw a group sitting on the porch of one of the cabins in rocking chairs. Molly, Kate, Sophie, Mason, and James sat watching the two of them walk to the cabin without a word. The five counselors gave each other the same look because they knew something wasn't right. Mason and James got up and started walking towards Moore and Barker's cabin.

"Where do you think you're going gentleman?" asked Sophie.

Mason whispered sarcastically, "To ask them for some cupcakes for the campers after dinner." Molly and Kate both looked at each other, then at Sophie, then at the boys.

"Really?" answered Sophie.

"No. We're going to figure out what they were doing back there this early," Mason replied. Molly and Kate looked at each other again and giggled at their conversation. Mason and James walked off to Barker and Moore's cabin. Meanwhile Sophie looked at Kate and Molly giving them the evil eye.

Molly, Kate, and Sophie are triplets. If that tells you anything about their life. They were all adopted by a young married couple with one child of their own. Every summer, since they were five years old, they went to the same summer camp they work at now. Once they started to get older they were able to become CIT's and then promoted to counselors. Now they each have their own group of campers. Because they aren't identical triplets people have a hard time figuring out that they are triplets. Kate is the oldest triplet. She has dark brown hair, 5'5" light freckles across her face. She likes to dress casually, jeans, t-shirts, stuff like that. She's a very laid back kind of person. Molly, the middle triplet, the shortest of the three at 5'4" with light brown hair, green eyes, and freckles covering her nose and cheeks. Her style of clothing you could say would also be like Kate's, jeans, tees and tank tops, but usually has her hair in a braid, ponytail, or pulled back in some way. And then there's Sophie. God love her, but she's one of the girls that likes to get her beauty sleep and cleans up very nicely. Her style is all about color coordinating and matching metals. She is the youngest of the three girls and one of those girls who can pull a lot of guys. A blonde, with blue eyes, and such a clear complexion that no freckle lays on her face.Sophie is the one who is closer with their adopted mother. She's one of the women who is very organized and kind of a neat freak. Molly and Kate though, are closer with their adopted dad. For a living, he bails hay and slotters pigs and cattle. The two of them love to help and watch him when he's working.

Mason and James get over to Barker and Moor's cabin. When they walked up the stairs to the porch, they knocked on the door. No answer, so Mason knocked on the door again. Barker opened the door, annoyed, with a shovel in his hand.

"Go wake up all the campers and have them go to the mess hall. Once you get up there, don't let anyone leave, including yourselves. We'll be back in a little bit." Barker said while Moore was scrambling in the room behind him grabbing stuff from all over the room and putting it by the door.

"Why?" James asked.

"Where are you going? Why do you have a shovel? Why

can't we leave the mess hall? And what is Moore doing?" Mason questioned.

"There's something in the woods on a trail we really don't want any of the campers to see and we'd prefer if you didn't know what it is either. Okay?" Barker snapped. He and Moore stood in the doorway of the cabin looking at Mason and James. The boys walked back to the girls and told them they needed to get the campers up and ready to go to the mess hall as soon as possible.

They split up and went to the cabins to get the campers. While they were running around trying to get ready, the five of them stood outside of the cabins with each other waiting. After breakfast, all the campers went back and sat at their tables talking to each other, too busy to question why they were still there. An hour later, however, the campers started to question things and thought they could do whatever, so they decided to test Molly, Kate, Sophie, Mason, and James' patience. They started getting really loud, running around, and then wanted to play tag. As they were running and pushing tables and chairs out of the way, a horn blew. The campers ran out of the mess hall and found a hat outside of the door. It was the same hat that Moore was wearing when he and Barker left to go to the woods. One of the campers picked it up and when James walked up to him he took it from the kid and showed Mason and the girls. The horn blew again.

Everyone looked at each other after a group of girls screamed. A group of boys ran over to where they heard the horn sound come from. That's when all the campers screamed. They stood there in shock, not knowing what to do next. Everyone then began to panic, wondering how this could have happened. Moore and Barker were placed the same way the little girl from the woods was. Gutted and hung. None of the campers recognized who they were until they looked closely at their blood covered faces. Some of the campers ran back inside of the mess hall because the sight of the men made them sick to their stomachs. Molly and Kate turned to all of the campers and told them all to go back inside the mess hall because they didn't want them out while Mason and James went over to them trying to process what was happening and think of how to clean the mess up.

Once Molly, Kate, and Sophie got all of the campers back in the mess hall the kids were freaking out. Mason and James stood out by Moore and Barker's dead bodies. They cut them both down from the branch they were hanging from and laid them softly on the ground next to the tree.

"Well, what are we going to do about this?" James asked Mason while they both had a confused look on their faces.

"I have no idea," replied Mason, standing there with his hands on his hips, looking at both of the men that left alive less than two hours ago.

"Boys, you need to figure out what to do with them before campers just start running out here." Molly said, walking down the small hill from the mess hall to the tree where they were standing.

"If these kids see them one more time, who knows what they're going to do," Kate said walking next to Molly.

"Wait if you two are right here, then where's Sophie?" James asked while pointing at the both of them and looking back behind them at the mess hall. Sophie ran out of the mess hall, looking like she had just seen a ghost.

"I stepped into the kitchen for one second. So tell me what just happened there and why I just saw half the kids dead on the floor?" She says looking out of breath and continuing to turn her head back between the mess hall and them. Molly, Kate, Mason, and James looked at her as if she was crazy.

"What did you just say?" Mason said with a scoff in his voice and a confused look on his face.

"I said," Sophie continued hysterically, "a bunch of the campers are dead, just lying there on the floor, dead." They all gave her the same look, like she had to have been seeing things. Molly and Kate looked at each other and Mason and James looked at each other.

They all ran inside the mess hall to find a figure dressed in black with a bulky knife in his hand. He turned around, looking at them with a smirk on his face. Standing there before the dead kids on the floor, the girls' dad said, "I started this camp. I made up those stories. Now the old camp stories are true. So, who wants to go next?"

PEACE MACHINE

LOGAN MARSH

Inspired by Georgia O'keeffe's painting "Blue and Green Music"

Everybody knew that the world was split in two, Blue and Green. The insignificant lives of the many outweigh the long living fruitful lives of the few, John knew this better than anyone. Now, staring into death's eyes at the end of his short life, he only has one purpose, to feed the Machine.

Nobody knew when the Machine gained total control but everyone knew of its inception. Legends say that around the 21st century, during the third world war, all the nations came together to make an AI to stop the carnage going on around them. It's solution, everyone picks a side. The Machine promised peace for all as long as it was obeyed, and for centuries this was known, this godless and meaningless planet known as Earth had one savior, the Machine.

John knew that Blue was the righteous side and Green was the wrong side, this was taught to him at a young age, and knew that all of his hatred of the Greens would be bottled up into him and released into the Machine in just a couple hours. He woke up, ate breakfast, showered, and was on his way to the Blue Headquarters, to fulfill his destiny. The Blue District of the last remaining city on Earth was bustling as it usually is, with people going in all directions imaginable, kids wandering, and a riot or two, it was all normal and mundane to him. The people of the last remaining city only felt three emotions, hate, greed, and anger, all directed toward the Green portion of the city. No one ever ventured there, for fear of being mauled to death by people vouching for their righteous side.

Throughout human history, everyone's thoughts on life and this world could be boiled down to two categories, though those categories are always changing. Good vs. evil, Coke vs. Pepsi, religion, politics, mostly meaningless things people would fight over all for some pointless conjecture and dominance. The Machine knew that this is what separates man and animal, and thus split the world in two using the thing that every human could relate to and fight for, Music. When the Machine is fed by those who believe in the righteous side of the Green or the Blue, music is made. Music that keeps people going, keeps people happy, when the people of the last city hear the Music of the Machine they are reminded why they live, and thus, want the Machine to keep making it.

Despite this everyone must pick a side, from the ages of 4 to 15, everyone represents their preferred music. John would be Blue until he drew his last breath, he was sure of it, as he passed all the same familiar places that he did as kid, he was reminded why he was fighting the good fight. It was just a fact to John at this point, their way of life was wrong and ours was the path the Machine wanted us to follow. He kept thinking to himself as he made his way to the headquarters of the Blue that his life was meaningless if not for the Machine. He had no friends, no family, nothing but the clothes on his back, and the apartment he lived in to call his own. John hated everyone and everything including himself, the only person he had some compassion for was the little girl on the third block of the last city.

Penny is a special kid, she has wide eyes, pigtails, and brown hair. She was thrown out of the Green subdivision a couple of years ago, the Blue officers thought of her as just one more person to feed the Machine and end this godforsaken war so she was adopted into the Blue subdivision at the age of four. She is viewed as the " village weirdo" by everyone. She has never expressed any of the normal emotions felt by people of the righteous path, while some civilians are able to go on long elaborate essays about their way of life, Penny has never spoken of either side.

Many thought she would never be able to fit in seeing as she was from the Green side. People at first tried to teach her of their ways, how to worship the Machine and become a good feeder, but Penny never seemed to grasp that concept. All she does every day is try to plant flowers on a little patch of soil near her apartment. In a world where people worship a Machine, nature is hard to come by in the last city, many people going their whole lives never even seeing a branch from a tree. Penny would go out every day and watch them grow, whispering to herself

"We all are going to go someday".

Everyone hated her. People kept her around as either a source of comedy or just another reason to hate the Green side. People would throw rocks at her, stomp her flowers, and thrash her pretty much every day. With all the bruises that she had she was nearly unrecognizable some days. Blood dripping from her face, tears in her eyes, and dead flowers were all products of going against the Machine.

John sees Penny every day on his walk. Rain, snow, drought, it didn't matter, she was always there. He turned at all the same spots and passed all the same people and places on his way to her house, and when he finally made it, she wasn't there. No one there, only a white tulip sprouting from the ground. Looking down at the flower, John realized how small it truly was, an insignificant little speck of life compared to him.

"Why on Earth does Penny give a damn about a stupid little flower," John thought to himself as he crushed it. He thought maybe it was a kid thing and tried to recall childhood memories of his.

He was 15 now, his parents were fed at a young age, and he had to live on his own. He never remembers doing any of what Penny did when he was young. Don't get him wrong, John hated Penny as much as the next guy, but there was something so innocent and naive about her, that made John disappointed to not see her today. But it didn't matter, today he would say goodbye to all of that as he fed the Machine. Penny was too young to understand anything of significance. Unlike Penny, John had a grasp on his life.

At that moment, exactly noon on a Sunday right when John arrived at the headquarters, the music started playing. It only plays once a month and everyone savors the moment. John saw pedestrians stop in their tracks, drop their suitcases and possessions, get on the ground, and listen. As the clock struck on the headquarter's clock, the heavenly symphony that the savior of the Earth had to offer started playing. John sat down on the steps of the building and listened, he imagined a warmth that he never had from his parents, friends he never made, happiness he never achieved. He started crying, John had waited for this moment all of his life, it had finally arrived, it was finally here. All the cruelty of this world, the violence he sees on the streets, the hatred, it would all be a distant memory soon. For the first time in his life, John was happy. He cried and rocked himself back and forth knowing it would all be over soon, he wouldn't have to be a burden anymore, and he wasn't going to continue being just another mouth to feed for the people of the Blue district. As the song played, he finally had a purpose.

Others cried and wept around him, hugging themselves and smiling. And, then just as quickly as it began, the song ended and everyone wiped their faces and went about their day. John wiped the tears from his face, got up, and faced the future that was in store for him. He approached the doors of the building. It had a poster on it that said "Our numbers are down, consider feeding today." The poster had a smiling woman on it with blonde hair, Blue eyes, and nearly every piece of her outfit had the emblem of the Machine and a tint of Blue to it. John opened the door and was soon stuck in a long line of people, all here for the same reason.

John waited and waited, and waited, and reflected on his life, what little of it he truly had. He had woken up and done the same mundane and meaningless things that everyone had done in this city. Nobody in this city ever did anything of significance, nor did they ever have any fun or happiness in their life. John couldn't remember the last time he smiled, besides of course when the music was playing. It always seemed like John was pulled out of his life when it started playing, like a bird flying away, he too leaves his body for just a couple moments every time it plays. He imagined death would be much the same, no more of this world, no more hate, no more Penny, Just him and the Machine. It sounded like paradise, but then the music stops, and he's back.

"Can I help you?" A lady asked him, taking John out of his own little world.

"Yeah, I'm on the list to be fed today." She started looking around her desk for a piece of paper. The lady looked as if she was trying to pull off the same look as the lady on the poster; it was just not working. She had blue all over her as expected but her hair really didn't match her clothes at all. Not that it matters, this lady was one of the last people anybody saw before death, what she wore was hardly anyone's concern.

"John Morgan, scheduled for noon, is this you?"

"Uh, yeah that's me"

"Go through the door and shut it on your way out, say hi to the Machine, and follow his instructions, thank you, and have a nice day." The lady said half-heartedly as she turned back to her computer. With this final registration, John had nothing more to do, see, feel, or become, he had burned all of his bridges and was ready for his destiny. So why, he kept asking, did he do what he did next?

"Hey, um could you do me a favor? There's this little girl on the third block... could you tell her that... Well, tell her that she should really consider the cause we're fighting for."

The woman thought to herself first and then said

"Oh, you mean Penny? She killed herself this morning"

"What?"

"Yeah, that weird girl with the pigtails, she jumped off a building this morning. The police were getting ready to kick her out of the Blue district this morning and they found her on the other side of town like that."

"Oh, well...Nevermind then"

"What a shame, huh? One more body to feed the Machine never goes to waste, but if you ask me-" The woman leaned in closer and whispered "that kid was the village weirdo, a little Green blotch in an otherwise perfect blue city"

"Ha ha, uh yeah, well thanks anyway"

"Whatever" The woman went back to work as if nothing happened, as if she didn't just crush the man standing in front of her's only When he had nothing left to do John thought, he thought as he walked to the Machine. Why did he ask that lady to talk to Penny? He knew more than anyone that Penny was hopeless, nothing would ever change her, as fast and frequent this world changes Penny would always remain a constant. So, why did he ask such a stupid question? More importantly, why did he care? Him and Penny had never even said anything to each other, hell, Penny probably didn't know he existed. That little twerp on the third block did nothing for anybody, she never loved nor hated anything or anyone, and John didn't like knowing that a person like that was gone. Even though it didn't matter, even though the Machine was his future, even though the Blue music would ring a month from now like nothing happened at all, John missed Penny.

"Well, we all gotta go someday." he kept thinking to himself as he closed the door to the Machine's room.

John was now standing in a dark hallway, pipes on the walls leading to the only source of light he could see, a turquoise block of light at the end of the hallway through a little doorway. He felt the rusty old pipes along the walls as he walked, the dials, buttons, lights, and screws were all foreign to him, technology from the past. He could hear a faint rendition of the Blue music coming from the end of the hallway, compelling him. It was much softer than the rendition he heard this morning, much brighter and slightly faster as well. He tried to think of all the things he would say to the Machine, all the ways he would thank him for giving peace to the world, that despite the low numbers of people, Blue would triumph.

Trying to hold back tears of joy from the beautiful tune he heard, he made his way down to the hallway, stepped through the door, and saw the Machine for the first time. Unlike the machinery leading him there, the Machine seemed to be this chrome, nearly mirror-like giant figure. It was lit up with this beautiful sea Green color that moved as if they were waves in the ocean, with what seemed like brush strokes of black at the tips of each color, making it seem like the Machine had this depth to it. "A sea of cool colors and symphony of souls" is what the Machine was described as. He had no eyes, for he saw all, nor did he have any other human-like features, except for a tiny little doggy door at the bottom of the Machine. It was rusty and bent, you could see sharp spikes, girders, and rods move inside the doggy door. Other than this little detail the Machine was heavenly, no, it was heaven itself, the more John looked at the more he wanted to help it, the more he wanted to serve his purpose.

"*Hello, John, how are you*?"

The Machine said this in a calm and friendly voice, like an old high school buddy that you would walk into after not seeing them for years. John was shaking in his blue shoes, he didn't know how to respond, all while this heavenly music played in the background. It all just seemed so perfect, he had never been happier.

"*You seem to be anxious. Do not be afraid, this process will be over soon.*"

"I... thank you, thank you so much for everything you have given me, I love you"

"*You are welcome. Come now, we haven't much time to lose.*"

John stepped closer to the Machine, a smile on his face, he was ready for whatever was to come next.

"*Good, now get in a crawling position and crawl through the small window in front of you.*"

Doing as he was told, he got a good look at what was through the doggy door, he saw blood everywhere, not a single spot not covered in a red paint-like substance. He could see another doggy door on the other side, he assumed is was for the Green district's side, seeing as their headquarters shared the same building. He was scared, he thought this would be a little quicker and painless.

"Is this going to hurt, Machine?"

"*No, it will not hurt, it will be over before you know it, now get in a crawling position and crawl through the small window in front of you*"

"Ok... and uh thanks again for everything you have done,

I mean if it was for you I would have shot myself or something. You have given me a greater purpose, thanks."

"*You are welcome. Now get in a crawling position and crawl through the small window in front of you.*"

John took a deep breath and did as he was told he got to die listening to his favorite song, with a smile on his face, and finally feeling as if he was happy.

However, this was a lie. The truth is that John's life was stolen from him, stolen from him by an insecure and scared society worshiping a byproduct of a bloodier war than the little body-chopping doggy door room that John was now in. He had served his purpose in this life, in another he was a husband and a father to the family he loved, in another he was a chef, a doctor, a veterinarian, a teacher you name it. John could have been somebody, but he wasn't. The Machine was still standing though, and it would continue to eat the depressed, hopeless Johns of this pointless and meaningless, for years and years as Pennys come and go. The Machine would feed on both sides of the city for centuries and centuries until all the flowers were stomped, all the secretaries have gone, and no more pain existed in the world. The Machine would feed until there was nothing but him, and Blue and Green music.

WE GO TOGETHER

NICKOLE MARTIN

Inspired Edward Hopper's painting "Summer Evening"

The neighborhood was dark, rainy, hazy, the streets felt narrow, and the houses looked like they had been abandoned. Seemed usual for the outskirts of downtown Chicago. We all sat at the table eating the meal our mother had prepared for us. I just picked at it and pushed it around on my plate. She mostly buys the cheapest thing she can find and slops it together. There was an uneasy presence at the table. While we all sat there in silence my phone started buzzing. I glanced down at my phone. It was Jacob. He wanted me to meet him outside.

"I'll be back," I said as I got up, not making any eye contact and pushing in my chair.

"Chloe..." My mother started to speak as the door shut but I met Jacob outside and we started walking.

"Are you hungry?" Jacob said with a smile on his face.

"Starving!" I shouted with a flirty laugh and grin on my face. Jacob has known me pretty much my whole life. We met in first grade. Jacob had curly blonde hair that reminded me of golden rays of sun. He had eyes bluer than the ocean. I could get lost in them for hours. Jacob's dad is never there and his mom works all the time so he doesn't see her very often. We ordered some food at the pizza place up the road. We got our food and headed up for the roof. We laid there on the roof eating our pizza and just looking at the stars. Looking at the stars you can almost see the reflection of what our lives used to be like before things went south. We sat there silently for a little bit just eating and I finally broke the silence.

"Do you ever think we will find happiness?" He stopped for a second.

"What do you mean?"

I just rolled my eyes, laughed, and said, "Do you ever think we will find love and just live a happy life?" You could see the sadness in his eyes. He had this sad look on his face. He scooted closer to me and began to speak.

"Of course I do. Everyone has someone out there for them." My heart was racing. I had butterflies in my stomach.

"Yeah, I guess you're right," I said, attempting to sound calm. We started off back to his house. With my dad being in jail my family wasn't doing good so I tried to not be home.

We got to Jacob's house, walked in, and he went to the fridge. He grabbed a couple beers, his pack of cigarettes, and then we headed upstairs. I sat down on the bed next to him as he lit a cigarette. Something felt different. I thought to myself that there was a stronger connection between us. Was I falling for him? Of course I was. We had been best friends forever. We know every secret about each other. I began to cry with tears just pouring. Jacob put his arms around me and held on to me while wiping the tears from my face.

"It's gonna be okay Chloe. It's gonna be okay." He whispered in my ear in a gentle voice.

I could feel his emotions as his words brushed through my ear. His arms around me gave me a sense of relief. I pulled myself together and he handed me his cigarette. I got up and turned off the light. I laid down next to him and felt a sense of security as I drifted off to sleep. Morning came and I was still tired but I had a long shift at work. I opened my eyes and they felt heavy and dry. The crying and being exhausted had really started to take a toll on me. I woke Jacob up and I went to go get my shower before work. As I'm getting in the shower Jacob went downstairs to make us breakfast. I turned on the water and locked the door. I stood in the shower with the warm water hitting my face. It was very relaxing. It felt like my pain was numbed for a brief moment. I got out of the shower and threw on a t-shirt Jacob had and headed downstairs. He made bacon, sausage, eggs and biscuits. I could smell it all before I even opened the door. It felt like I was a kid again and waking up to the smell of breakfast our mom and dad were cooking in the kitchen. I looked at myself in the mirror seeing myself as a kid smiling and our family being happy and laughing together. I opened the door and walked downstairs to the table. Jacob was sitting there waiting for me. He looked at me and smiled as we began to eat. Once I finished my food I went back upstairs to get ready. I threw on my clothes and lit myself a cigarette. I was so anxious and stressed because of my family. I knew I had to leave so I headed downstairs where again Jacob was waiting on me.

"Are you ready?" Jacob asked.

"Yes." I said with a grin on my face. We walked out the door and started off down the street. We made it to my work. I worked at the pizza place just up the road from his house. He gave me a hug before he asked "I'll see you after work?"

"Yep," I said, trying to stay positive. We stood there for a second looking into each other's eyes. His eyes were the prettiest crystal blue. I could see myself in them. I couldn't help but see me and him together in his eyes.

"It's gonna be okay," Jacob said while he grabbed my face.

"I know," I stammered, still staring into his eyes. It was time for me to go inside. He gave me another hug before I had to go. I walked in and clocked in. I was getting everything ready for the afternoon rush turning on the ovens and placing supply orders. It had been about an hour and today had already felt like a long day. The afternoon rush finally arrived. I was busy taking orders and making sure people had what they needed. Before I knew it the rush was mostly gone. By that point I went and started unloading boxes in the back. I heard the front door slam. I was caught off guard at first when someone began to yell.

"Chloe! You better have the money!" A voice from the front shouted. My heart was racing. I didn't know what was going on. What money? Was it something to do with my mom or dad? I hid myself behind some boxes. He began shouting again.

"I'm going to get my money one way or another!" He shouted as he left. I sat there for a little while trying to figure out what was going on. I finally got back up and finished unloading the couple of boxes that were left. It was time for me to clock out. I went and clocked out and raced home. I opened the door to find my mom passed out drunk on the couch.

"What the hell mom?" I shouted waking her up from her drunk sleep. She looked at me kinda confused and disoriented, her brain not fully functioning yet. "You need to get it together and whoever you owe this money to, pay them back." You could hear the "What are you talking about?" she said, slurring her words.

"You or dad owe someone money. This guy came into my work today screaming about it and looking for me. They were very angry," I said in a stern tone. She just looked at me and went blank. I waited for a minute growing even more angry with her.

" Answer me!" I shouted. Still, she sat there blank and emotionless. Tears began to fall from my eyes. I was so angry.

"You all are the worst parents. You both have wasted your lives and are nothing more than worthless! Dad's in jail and here you lay - a pathetic drunk who can't provide for the family!" Thoughts were rushing through my brain and I threw my paycheck at her.

"Pay them back!" I yelled as I stood there still crying and angry.

"Enough!" She screamed reaching for her long neck bottle. She raised her arm back, throwing the bottle at me. I felt the broken glass pierce my skin. It started to bleed and burn. I ran out of the house. I could still hear her yelling but I wasn't able to make out what she was saying with the anger running through me. I grabbed my phone from my pocket and saw I had a bunch of missed messages from Jacob. I called him and he met me outside of my house. He ran to me and wrapped his arms around me. His arms were a safe place for me. They held me tight making me feel like no trouble could possibly reach me. He held me for a second as I was standing there crying still and then he said, "I'm going to go pull the truck around. I want you to tell me everything."

He brought the truck around and he helped me get in. I sat in the truck replaying everything in my head still just trying to process it. We stopped by the store so he could buy me some bandages for my wounds. I couldn't help but wish they made something to heal the internal wounds my family had created. The pain from my family had become too much. I became more depressed and had really intrusive thoughts. We finally made it back to his house and he carried me inside to his kitchen. I was still a mess. I was frozen in a way that made me feel almost nonexistent but still there. Jacob went to grab the peroxide to clean out my wounds. I looked at my reflection in the shiny silver fridge they had in their kitchen. I didn't realize how bad my injuries were. As I looked at my reflection It was like half of me was the younger me and the other half was me standing there in Jacob's kitchen. All the pain came back. I felt so weak. The pain was so sharp and hit me so quick I just collapsed on the floor. Jacob rushed down the stairs and picked me up. He pulled out a chair and sat me down. He started removing the glass from my skin. He began to pour peroxide on the open wounds. I felt the peroxide hit my skin. A rushing pain took over my body but I was so weak I couldn't make a sound. Once he cleaned me all up he helped me upstairs to bed and we both knew I would tell him everything after I slept.

Jacob called my work telling them I would be out for a couple days. I just rested for the days I had off. He was taking care of me making sure I had everything I needed. He brought me some warm freshly made breakfast and brought me some water. He sat it on the side table next to his bed. He crawled into the bed with me and brushed his hands through my hair. I was awake but I didn't want to move. It was very relaxing to me. Jacob gave me a kiss. It was so gentle and you could just feel the connection between us. I opened my eyes. He just looked at me and smiled. I picked up my plate and ate the food he made me. As the next couple days went by I started to feel a little better. It was time for me to go back to work. I went to sleep that night next to Jacob. He just played with my hair as I lay there trying to fall asleep. I finally dozed off. Even though things had been getting better I had this feeling things weren't gonna stay like that for long. It's what my grandma used to always call "going good blues."

I got up the next morning and got ready for work like I normally did. I arrived at work, clocked in, started getting tables ready and then we opened. It was super busy so it went by pretty fast for once. But I had this bad feeling. I'd had it for a few days now but I couldn't pinpoint what could possibly be wrong. I needed to go to my house after work and talk to my mom. I was dreading it. I texted Jacob letting him know that I was going to talk to my mom and that I would be a little late getting to his house. When I finished up my shift I walked to my house. I opened the door and to my surprise I didn't see my mom on the couch. I heard something coming from the back of the house. My mom's voice and this other voice. As I got closer to the voices it hit me. The guy who ran In screaming. I was up against the wall so they couldn't see me but I listened really close to hear what they were saying.

"This is all I have please I'll get you the rest later," My mom said in a distressed tone

"No, I have given you all time. Time is up. You pay me or I take something that you can't ever get back," he said with an evil grin on his face.

"You can't. Please don't take Chloe!" she said with panic in her voice. He just looked at her snickering. I realized I needed to get out of here. I took a step and they heard me. I panicked and I didn't know what to do. Should I run? Should I just not move? All these thoughts were running through my mind. It was overwhelming. They saw me standing there and started walking towards me. I was still frozen. As they got closer I saw the man had something in his hand. The man was big, muscular, and scary. He had tattoos and scars all over himself. As I looked closer to see what he had in his hand I saw it was a knife.

"Don't move," he said with a serious tone. My fight or flight had really set in and I took off. He grabbed me before I could even take two steps. His grip was so tight there was no escape. He held the blade to my throat. It was very sharp.

"This is what happens when you don't pay me the money you owe me back," he said, pushing the blade closer to my throat. As the knife hit my throat, Jacob had opened the door. I was still frozen. I couldn't even speak. Jacob saw me and stopped in his tracks. Tears swelled up in his eyes.

"No!" he shouted. "I love her, please don't." He started to tremble. The knife split my skin and I began losing sight of what was around me. I saw light and I was hearing voices.

"Come home! Come home! Come home!" the voices were saying. I saw the pearly gates that we used to talk about in Sunday school when I was a kid. Jesus was right there and I saw him reach his arm out to me. "Come on Chloe, let's go home. You're safe now." I grabbed his arms, shocked that they were a million times more comforting than Jacob's, and we walked through the gates into heaven.

EDGAR DEGAS' ABSINTHE DRINKER

JAGER MATTINGLY

The soft breeze brushes through Marie's long, auburn hair as she runs through the Magnolia trees engulfing her back garden. She runs gracefully, attempting to escape from the forever-lasting game of tag with her mother, Dorothy.

"You can't catch me!" Marie exclaims.

Marie's mother cuts through the floral trees, where she sits and waits for Marie to pass by; she sees her chance, jumps out of her hiding spot, and grasps Marie tightly.

"You caught me," Marie says, giggling.

"Alright, hun', let's go inside now; it's 'bout time for me to start supper."

Dorothy sets Marie down as they walk towards their one-bedroom home, the roof of gray slate shingles and the outer walls of white vinyl siding. They step on their tiny porch, opening the large mahogany door. The smell of the water-rotted hardwood floors flourishes throughout the home; they walk together through the small sitting area into the kitchen, where Marie assists her mother in beginning to make supper.

"Go on an' grab the eggs and the vegetable basket for me, hun'," Dorothy tells Marie.

"What'r we makin' mama?" She asks as she hands the ingredients to her mother.

"I'm tryna' make us somethin' small; we ain't got us much food left, and it's 'bout to be winter... I was thinkin' somethin' like some boiled eggs and vegetables."

"Do we got us enough stuff to make us some dessert after, mama?"

"I'm sure a small pie won't be a problem, hun'."

Marie fills their only pot with water from their well, throws it on the stove, and allows the water to boil; Dorothy then adds the chopped vegetables. As they sizzle in the pot, Marie sets the table. Their table had three chairs, but only two were filled. Marie's father left them four years ago; Marie was only one, so she has only seen her father through old family portraits. Dorothy never showed her struggle to Marie, but enduring the harsh seasons without a husband was difficult.

Marie sets down the tablecloth along with the table mats and bowls where they will place their food. The two candles in the middle of the table burn bright in the light-lacking home; the two windows at the front of the house and the single oil lamp only offer minimal light. She grabs some of their only Tupperware, the two metal spoons she sets next to their bowls.

"Tables done, mama," Marie says.

"Looks good, hun', come on an' help me start up this pie... I'm 'bout to go on an' take out these vegetables and throw in them eggs."

"Okay, mama," Marie responds.

Marie walks towards the kitchen, the floors creaking with each step. She grabs the ingredients for the pie on her way: apples, sugar, flour, cinnamon, butter, and salt. Marie sets the ingredients on the counter next to her mother.

"Thanks, hun'."

Dorothy places the eggs in the pot while Marie starts creating the dough for the pie. Marie mixes a large bowl of butter, salt, sugar, flour, and some shortening for extra flavor. While the eggs are boiling and Marie continues on the dough, Dorothy begins filling the pie; she mixes the sliced apples and brown sugar, and as she shakes in the leftover cinnamon, she adds the softened butter. She combines until the apples are completely covered in the cinnamon filling.

"We work pretty well together, don't we, Marie?" Dorothy asks.

"Yes," Marie says, laughing.

Dorothy grabs the well water they had saved and previously boiled to remove any bacteria; she pours it into two cups and walks over to the table, setting one next to Marie and one next to her bowl.

"Thank you," Marie exclaims.

"You're welcome, hun'," Dorothy replies.

Picking up their spoons, they dip them into the steaming vegetables and eat.

"They need some salt, don't they," Dorothy asks

"Maybe a little, but they taste good, Mama."

Dorothy grabs the salt and pepper from the center of the table and lightly sprinkles it on her vegetables. She grabs her spoon and tries them again.

"Much better!" She exclaims

The smell of apple pie is prominent throughout the home. Dorothy stands up, cleans up the dirty dishes left behind from dinner, and stacks them on the counter.

"The pie smells like it's 'bout done, don't it?" Dorothy asks.

"Yes!" Marie says excitedly.

Dorothy grabs her oven mitts and takes the pie out of the oven. The crust is golden, with the apple filling trying to push its way through the top; the steam hits Dorothy's face as she removes the pie from the cookstove. She sets it on the counter, grabs her pie cutter, and slices it into 6 medium-sized pieces. Dorothy grabs two slices of pie, falling apart as she tries to place them on the plate; she takes them over to the table, where Marie waits patiently.

"This looks so good, Mama."

Dorothy sits as Marie begins to eat; Dorothy grabs her fork, cuts a piece of the pie off, and raises it to her mouth, blowing it so she doesn't get burnt. The pie is finally cool enough; she puts the pie in her mouth, beginning to chew and enjoying every second.

"I think this is our best pie yet!" Dorothy says with her mouth still full.

"I think so, too!" Marie replies.

As the sun sets, the light in the house lessens every minute, the candles go out, and Dorothy tells Marie it's time for bed.

"Are you ready for bed, Marie?" Dorothy asks.

"Yes, mama," Marie replies.

Marie changes into her nightgown and lays on the queen-sized bed she and her mother share. Dorothy changes into her nightgown as well; she inserts herself into the bed along with Marie, and they talk about their day. Dorothy looks to her left and sees Marie's eyes are shut.

"Goodnight, hun'," Dorothy says

"Goodnight, Mama," Marie says with her eyes still closed.

Dorothy closes her eyes as well, Marie's small, cold feet touching her legs. She tucks herself deeper into the floral quilt that covers their bed. After a few minutes, Dorothy and Marie finally fall asleep.

"I'm home, mama!" Marie shouts

"Hey hun', how was your day?" Dorothy asks

"It was alright; it was slow at the bakery today. How was your day?"

"The same as every other day since I went to the doctors."

Fifteen years passed. Marie had gotten a job at a local bakery close to their home in Montgomery, Alabama. She had to start providing for them; eight years ago, Dorothy became very sick and has yet to overcome it. Because of this, Dorothy has been unable to provide. Marie has been attempting to help since she was twelve years old, scraping up any extra money. Marie begins to walk towards the sitting area, flopping down on the torn-up couch, the floors still creaking. Dorothy sits in the chair adjacent to her; Dorothy begins coughing. She looks down and sees her hands covered in a thick, red liquid. Blood.

"Are you okay, Mama?" Marie asks urgently

"I'm okay. It's just getting worse every day."

Marie bounces up and goes to the kitchen to grab a rag for her mom, stepping over the crooked nails sticking out of the hardwood floors. She hurried back to her mom's care.

"Thank you, hun'," Dorothy says while still coughing.

Dorothy wipes the drying blood off her hands, and then the blood is still dripping from her mouth. Dorothy becomes nauseous from the sudden blood loss, trying her hardest to stay awake. She continues to cough, more blood leaking from each hack, wiping the blood while the rag is already soaked.

"Can you bring me a glass of water, hun'?" Dorothy asks through her cough.

Marie hurriedly ran to the kitchen, grabbing the pot of

already boiled water and pouring it into a glass before quickly taking it back to her mother, not spilling a drop.

"Thank you."

Marie sits down on the couch, the couch squeaking as she sinks deeper into it. Dorothy's coughing seemingly comes to an end.

"Are you okay, mama?" Marie asks

"I should be fine." "That was probably the worst fit I've had," Dorothy replies, still out of breath.

"Just watch yourself, don't let it get too bad, mama." "It's getting late; we should probably get going to bed, mama."

Marie walks towards the kitchen, blowing out the two candles illuminating the darkness. Marie grabs her favorite nightgown, tosses it on, and heads to bed; Dorothy does the same. They cuddle together in bed and throw on every quilt they have, trying to stay warm on this cold night. Dorothy continues to cough throughout the night, but after each one, she just goes back to sleep. It's about midnight, and Marie wakes up to go to the outhouse-they couldn't afford a bathroom in their home. She finishes using the restroom, steps out of the outhouse, and hears something peculiar. She slowly walks into the house and quietly opens the door; it is her mother. Her mother is suffocating; the blood from her cough is sitting in her throat and has put her body in shock. She is unable to move. Marie runs to her mother's aid.

"MAMA!" "MAMA!" "MAMA, PLEASE!"

Marie shakes her mother, slowly seeing life leave her eyes. Marie flips Dorothy on her stomach, and blood begins to ooze from her mouth, but it is too late. The blood had entered her airway, causing trauma and a lack of oxygen to the brain. Dorothy was dead. Marie continued shaking her mother, hoping and praying that some miracle would wake her. She flipped her over on her back; her body was becoming cold, Marie's hands shaking, and teardrops began to fall onto Dorothy's body. Wails of sadness begin to leave their home as Marie finally realizes what has happened. Dorothy Grove's body lay lifeless on the bed, her mouth open, blood still dripping out. Marie hugs her body.

"Mom... please... Just wake up, please, mama."

Marie lay by her mother's side for the rest of the night; she didn't sleep, and her face was hurting from crying, but every time she looked over, more tears rolled down her face. After eight hours, Marie realizes she needs to get her mother's body out of their house. She uses their single horse and buggy and, with much effort, places her mother's body in the wagon and rides to her church. As she arrives at the church, she asks the Priest about options for her mother's body. He recommends burying her under the church and planning a funeral. The Priest assists Marie by carrying her mother's body inside, laying it in one of the many hospital beds in the back of the church. The Priest bows his head down and says a prayer.

"Lord Jesus, holy and compassionate: forgive her sins. By dying, you unlocked the gates of life for those who believe in you: do not let our sister be parted from you, but by your glorious power, give her light, joy, and peace in heaven where you live and reign forever and ever. Amen."

"Amen," Marie replies

The Priest covers her body with a thin white sheet as Marie says her final goodbyes. Marie walks out the door into the large open room, going through the aisles of seats, wherein one of the seats, a man in a black suit and top hat, sits. The man's tired, dark eyes make contact with Marie's; looking forward and back at her, Marie walks up to this man.

"Hello, sir." "What is your name?" Marie asks.

"Greg." The man replies. "You are Marie?"

"Yes?" Marie questions. "How did you know my name?"

"I'm here for you, Marie."

Marie is immediately taken aback; her mother has just died, and now a random man has shown up. Marie hears the large door in the back squeak as it opens; the Priest steps through and begins walking towards Marie, his Oxfords clacking against the floor with every step he takes.

"Why are you still here, Marie?" the Priest inquires.

Marie looks back at the seats, seeing the man peer through his hat at the Priest.

"I was talking to this man," Marie replies.

"What, man?"

Marie steps out of the way and presents the man to the Priest.

"Marie?" The Priest questions

"Yes, sir?"

"There is no one there, sweetheart." The Priest replies.

Marie looks at the Priest and looks back at the seats again. The man was sitting there with a menacing grin, placing a pipe in his mouth and smoke leaving the end.

"What do you mean you don't see him?...He's right there," Marie says.

The Priest continues to look at Marie, confused.

"I think you should go sit down, Marie... I think your mother's death is getting to your head...You're hallucinating."

Marie is scared at this point. She gets closer to the man and notices a heavy weight on her shoulders the closer she gets to the man. The man is still smiling, taking the pipe out of his mouth every once in a while.

"I think I'm gonna go then," Marie says.

"I think you should rest, Marie." "It'll be the best for you."

Still confused, Marie clenches her fist as she walks out, aggravated that the Priest couldn't see that man.

Marie opens the large, heavy door where she exits the church; she hops on her horse and buggy and rides down the dirt path toward the city. Marie notices a feeling weighing down on her. Marie whips her head to the right and sees Greg.

"What are you doing here?" Marie asks intensely.

"I must follow you," Greg replies.

Marie is frightened by this comment; she scoots over to the edge of her seat, as far away from him as possible. Marie still feels a groggy feeling, even more so when she looks at him. They continue to ride the dirt road until they make it into the city, with Marie still pushed against the edge of the seat. She stops her horse in front of a corner bar called "Sam's Bar." Marie steps down from her buggy and ties her horse to a fence out front. Marie steps onto the sidewalk and begins walking towards the bar's door. She steps in, and the bell at the top of the door rings to notify the bartender that someone has walked in. Greg follows in behind her. Marie immediately locks eyes with the bartender, tall and clean. Marie instantly looks away but feels the bartender's stare as she walks towards a booth. She arrives at her booth, squeezing between the lines of tables, Greg still following her. Marie and Greg sit side by side and wait for the bartender to serve them. They sit there for about five minutes before they see the bartender walk towards them, his black tie pasted against his side as he walks.

"So what would you like today, Ma'am?" the bartender asks.

"I need an Absinthe, please, and keep them coming," Marie demands.

"Will do...What is your name?" The bartender asks, smiling.

"Marie," she replies, "And yours?"

"Sam... Sam Wilson."

"So you must be the owner of the bar then?"

"No, my father is... But he named it after me," Sam replies.

"That's pretty neat... Well, It's nice to meet you, Sam," Marie says

"You too... I'll get your drink right out."

Sam walks away, and Greg begins to stare at Marie, his eyes widening every second.

"I am a ghost," Greg says.

"What?" Marie replies.

"Ima' ghost, Marie... I'm in your head, Marie... Only you can see me."

"That makes no sense; ghosts aren't real." Marie snaps back.

"I'm no normal ghost... I'm Greg the Ghost." His voice cracks as he speaks.

Marie stares at Greg, confused. Other people stare at Marie, and muttering breaks out.

"Is she crazy?" One person says.

"Who is she talking to?" Another says.

Marie checks around the small bar, listening to the people and seeing all of the people staring at her. She then realizes that Greg may just be telling the truth. Sam brings Marie her Absinthe, filled to the brim; the green liquid seeps down the side of the glass.

"Thank you," Marie says.

Sam nods his head and walks away. Marie begins to sip on her drink, reminiscing on her memories with her mother, trying to forget what she saw earlier that morning, but no matter what, she just kept thinking of it, the blood, her mother's lifeless body, all of the memories came flooding back. Marie continues to drink the Absinthe until it is completely gone; she immediately asks for another, and then another, and another. Marie couldn't even think anymore. Greg sat there smiling the whole time. Greg enjoyed every moment of despair Marie had.

"Anyone wanna dance?" Marie stutters through her words.

Marie stands up, stumbling across the floor and grabbing Sam. She pulls him close and begins to dance to the band playing. Sam stares into her eyes, scared at first, but he gets more comfortable the longer they dance. Marie smiles as she looks up at him, forgetting everything that had happened that day, only focused on Sam. His bright blue eyes, dark, slicked-back hair, and tan skin make Marie feel something she had only ever felt from her mother. Love.

Greg silently walks up behind Marie; she feels his coarse beard on her shoulder. Marie immediately feels a heavy feeling again. However, Marie's intoxicated body brushed this off; she continued to dance with Sam, and other people began to join them until the bar broke out into a ballroom. Tables are moved from the center of the bar to the edges to create more space, and the band begins to play slow music. Greg, however, stands in the corner, watching Marie's every move. Greg doesn't like to see Marie having fun. He was there to ensure Marie was upset; Greg, seeing himself fail, made him bitter.

"Marie... psssst," Greg whispers.

Marie hears her name but is too sloshed to realize where she is hearing it from. Greg continues whispering her name until Marie finally catches on. She walks over to Greg, and he releases a heavy aura onto Marie. Marie is sober now and, once again, remembering that morning. It was like a videotape that kept replaying in Marie's head. Her mother's pale body, the coldness of her body, the blood dripping from her mouth; these thoughts were making Marie upset. Marie turns away from Greg and exits the bar, tears streaming down her face as she leaves. She mounts her buggy and begins to ride back towards their house. Sam steps outside of the bar door.

"Where are you going, Marie? We were just starting to have fun."

Marie didn't answer; instead, she rode off into the distance, following the same dirt road she took there back home. Once again, Greg was with her the whole way. This time, Marie accepted he was there; she didn't move away from him; she just sat there, stiff as a board.

Marie arrived home; she untied the spotted horse from the buggy and placed it back in its field. She then enters her home and flops down on her bed, still bloodstained from her mother. Marie realizes she needs to sleep. Without changing into her nightgown, she curls up into a fetal position on her bed, covering herself with her quilt, closes her eyes, and immediately falls asleep. Greg was still next to her, making sure his presence was known.

Months passed as Marie continued to go to the bar regularly, drinking her problems away. She would drink Absinthe every time she went, and in the small town, she was known as the "Absinthe Drinker." She continued to speak with Sam regularly. They began to form a relationship, and Sam finally asked Marie to go to a nice restaurant; Greg was still following Marie around. Marie and Sam go to dinner at 'Quasimotos' right across from the bar. The restaurant was candle-lit, with tons of tables lined up, each with a bouquet and tablecloth. Marie and Sam sat in the middle of the restaurant, and a waiter arrived at their table.

"What are you guys eating tonight?" the waiter asks.

"I think I'll have the lamb." "Cooked until slightly pink in the middle... I'll add water as well, please." Sam requests

"Alright... And for you, ma'am?"

"I'll just get the same," Marie replies.

"I'll get that right out."

Marie and Sam sit and wait for their food to arrive; they have small talk, Greg still lurking behind Marie. However, Marie notices that Greg is becoming less of a nuisance, and Marie doesn't feel as bad when he is around.

Marie and Sam's food finally arrives. They both place napkins in their laps and begin to feast.

"This is so good!" Marie exclaims

Marie and Sam finish their meals. Sam gets up to go to the front, where he pays for their food.

"Thank you," Marie says.

"Any time, hun'," Sam replies.

Marie's heart drops as he says this. Sam calling her hun' brings back all of the memories with her mother. A tear falls down her face, but she wipes it fast so no one notices.

As the sun sets, Sam walks outside, holding the door for

Marie. He climbs on his buggy and grabs Marie's hand to pull her up. Marie takes a giant step and mounts the wagon. Sam lashes the horses, and they begin to take off. Suddenly, Marie starts to cough. She covers her mouth with her hands. Pulling them back, she notices that her long white gloves are now stained red. Marie quickly sits on her hands so Sam doesn't see the blood. Sam arrives at Marie's home; he steps off the buggy and goes to the other side to assist Marie. Marie grabs his hand, forgetting she has blood on her hands; Sam notices this.

"What is this, Marie?"

"It's nothing," Marie replies.

"Is this blood?... Tell me the truth, Marie."

"Yes, it is."

Sam is immediately worried; he takes her inside, sitting with her until he believes she is okay. Before Sam leaves, he walks up to Marie hugs and kisses her on the forehead, he then exits through the large mahogany door.

Marie realizes she has the same symptoms as her mother and is scared to sleep. She remains awake all night, keeping a rag and water by her side.

Marie continues to cough, even through the morning, with blood occasionally coming out of her mouth. Marie gets up and decides it's time to prepare for the day. She notices a sharp pain in her chest; she grabs her chest and falls to the floor. Marie can't breathe. Marie fades in and out of consciousness until she finally sees a bright light coming from the door; Sam has come to check on her. Sam sprints to her assistance and finds that she is unconscious but still breathing. He attempts to sit her up so she can breathe, to no avail. Marie's heartbeat was quickly decreasing.

"I...Love...You"

Marie attempts to squeeze these words out. These words were her last. Marie Coolie was dead. Sam looked up in despair. Wails of pain left the house once again. Greg was still by Marie's side even until the end. Greg crouched down by Marie and kissed her on the forehead; Sam was still crying, looking at the ceiling. He finally looks back down at Marie and notices Greg's stocky body.

"Who are you?" "Get out, NOW!" Sam yells

"I was here for Marie... And now I'm here for you, Sam.. I shall not leave."

Sam begins to cry even louder than before, his heavy tears clapping against the hardwood floors. Sam attempts to punch Greg, but his fist passes right through. Greg smiles menacingly as Sam begins to connect the dots.

"You're the man Marie always spoke to... Truly...You're a... ghost."

Greg nods in affirmation. He gets up from the ground and walks over to Sam, Marie's lifeless body still lying on the floor. He sits next to Sam; the same heavy weight is now on Sam's shoulders.

Sam stands up from the floor, still staring at Marie; her eyes have lost all their light. Sam walks out the door, climbing on his horse and buggy to find help. Greg now follows Sam; Like Marie, Greg is all Sam's built-up sadness and grief.

Sam has now gone months without his love. He visited the church, and they set up a funeral for Marie. Marie was buried right next to her mother, Dorothy. Sam visits Marie's grave every day, bringing flowers each time. Whenever Sam goes, Greg sits there, waiting for him; Greg follows him. Greg finally tells Sam, "I am the eternal cycle of sadness."

THE APP

ADDIE MORGAN

Inspired by Edward Hopper's painting "Summer Evening"

I walked over to the window and stood as I watched my parents back out of the driveway. The car came to a halt and then quickly took off down the road. An excited feeling took over my body as I turned around and jumped down onto the sofa. I couldn't believe my parents actually left me here at the house by myself for the whole weekend. I was so excited, but what 15-year old wouldn't be? I mean I had the whole house to myself. No one to bother me, no one to tell me when I need to go to bed, life was great. But now that my parents are gone. I immediately texted my friend Emma that she could come over anytime now and to bring lots of snacks. My parents would actually kill me if they found out I was having someone over. It was one of the rules they had made before they left the house. Don't do anything stupid, don't leave the house, and don't have anyone over. I felt the vibration of my phone as it dinged, so I quickly picked it up. It was Emma saying she could come over in an hour or two and that she would text me when she left her house. That just got me even more excited about my weekend because Emma and I always had so much fun together no matter what we're doing. With me being an only child with parents who work a lot, it can get pretty lonely if I'm being honest. So Emma is basically the sister I never had. Now all I had to do was wait for her to get here.

As I sat slowly sinking into the sofa cushions, the silence of the empty house echoed. I would have thought being home alone would have been more fun and interesting. But honestly, I couldn't think of anything I wanted to do. As I sat there in my thoughts, the loud sound of my phone dinging ran through my ears. I quickly wondered who it could be since I knew it wasn't Emma saying she was on her way. It had only been a few minutes since I texted her. Maybe my mom or dad? I quickly reached for my phone that was sinking into the sofa next to me, and turned it on. It was a message, but just like I figured. Not from Emma or my parents. It was a message from Micheal Long. He was a guy I matched with months ago on a dating app I have. It was very unexpected, especially since I gave up on trying to find someone on that app a long time ago. Plus, I only got it because it felt like pretty much everyone in school was in a relationship but me. I mean even Emma had a boyfriend. Also, I've always wanted a boyfriend, and even more since Emma got one. I want someone I can have fun with like Emma does with her boyfriend. So honestly, dating someone from this app didn't sound like a bad idea. My eyes made their way down my phone screen and fixated on Micheal's message.

It read "Hey Claire, I think you're pretty. What do you think about getting together sometime?"

After reading that message, my mind went blank, my heart started to beat faster, and I could feel my face heating up. This can't be real. Is this actually happening? I just couldn't believe a guy, especially a guy like Micheal, thought I was pretty and even wanted to hang out. I can see it now. All the looks on everyone's face that made fun of me before, if they found out I could get with a guy like Micheal, oh that would feel so good. Just from the look of him from his profile makes my heart beat even faster, and I could bet he looks even better in person. He looks like a very mysterious guy and not to mention very good looking as well. My fantasizing came to a pause when I thought about how I was going to tell Emma about this. She's kind of protective over me when it comes to me dating because she doesn't want me to get hurt. She definitely wouldn't like the idea of me hanging out with a guy I met online. But on the other hand, she's my best friend. This is the kind of stuff I've been dying to talk to her about and now it's actually happening. After a few minutes of deep thought, I figured there's really no point in telling Emma about Micheal unless there is actually something to tell. Like this might lead to nothing. I mean there's no harm in that right?

I need to let Michael know I'm definitely down to hang out sometime. But when will I be able to hang out with him? I'm only 15 so I can't drive and my parents would never allow me to hang with him. Hell, they don't even know I have a dating app, and would probably lose it if they found out I did. All of this just made me feel like my head was spinning. But then I had a great idea. When am I ever going to home alone with my parents hours away again anytime soon? This weekend would be the perfect time to hang out with Micheal. But what about Emma? All I know is that I had to act fast with this great plan. So I grabbed my phone, clicked on Micheal's message and started to type away. After what seemed like forever I finally built up the courage to send it.

I replied, "Thanks Michael, and I would love to hang out with you. What about tonight?" I saw his typing bubbles appear and he quickly replied, "Yeah, sounds good. Send me your address and I'll meet you at your house around 8pm." I was more excited now than ever, but still very nervous. Next thing I knew after a little while of laying on the couch, Emma was pulling into my driveway. I must have been so into my show I missed her text. But I don't care, at least she's here. I went to the door and she came inside. We sat down and started talking, you know girl stuff. We played some games, watched a movie and made some cookies. I checked my phone after hearing it go off in the middle of our movie. It was Micheal, saying he was on his way. Crap I totally lost track of time and it was a quarter until eight. I needed to get Emma to leave, and fast. I thought for a second and came up with the quickest and most believable excuse I could think of. “Emma, today was really fun but I’m not really feeling the best right now. But we can definitely talk tomorrow!”

She said, “Don't worry, I was about to head out myself. But I hope you feel better, and yeah call me tomorrow!” She gathered her things and replied, “Thanks Emma and I will. Bye!”

“Okay, see ya,” she said and I sat up on the couch as Emma closed the door behind her and got in her car to drive away. Wow that was a lot easier to get her to leave than I thought. Then I realized he's going to be here any minute. I needed to get myself ready and actually look somewhat decent for once! I ran upstairs, put on some of my mom’s mascara and blush. I touched up my hair with the straightener and then ran to the closet to pick an outfit. I quickly remembered I had this one outfit Emma left at my house and she definitely has better style when it comes to clothes. I got it out and put it on. It was a matching pink top and skirt. Definitely more showy than the kind of clothes I normally wear but I felt really good in this outfit. I was adjusting the skirt when I heard the doorbell ring. I ran downstairs and paused in front of the door for a second, took a deep breath, and reached for the door handle. I opened the door and the dim light shining from behind him casted a tall shadow over me. He was a lot taller than I expected, at least a foot or two taller than me. But his looks definitely didn't disappoint and I was right. He did look even better in person.

"Hey Claire, good to get to see you in person."

I stuttered as I was searching for my words."Uh, oh yeah you too . . .Why don't you come on in? I can put on a movie or we can do whatever."

"Okay, yeah sounds good," Micheal said.

We made our way to the couch and sat down. There was a cushion length of distance between us but that didn't last long. After about 30 minutes into some random movie I put on we were shoulder to shoulder. Our two bodies connecting at our sides. I could feel him slowly breathing in and out. Finally he did what I have been dreaming of a guy to do for years. He reached out above his head, placing his arm around me. He slightly gripped the side of my arm with his hand and pulling me closer to his chest. I could feel his heartbeat, but it was nowhere near how fast mine was beating. The movie came to an end and we sat up on the couch and looked at each other. I noticed that it was quite dark outside so I turned my head to look at the clock on the stove. It was already almost 9:30pm. Time was flying by. Michael noticed me looking at the time. He tapped my shoulder, so I turned and directed my sight towards him. We locked eyes and just sat there for a second. I felt the tension between us and he got closer. Next thing I know he was grabbing the side of my face pulling us both in towards one another. Our lips met and we kissed. Multiple times. A shock of adrenaline ran through my body with each kiss. We pulled away from each other and both smiled.

"Wanna go and hang out on the porch before it gets too late?" asked Michael.

"Yeah, we can," I said, with the biggest grin on my face.

We walked out on the porch and it was the perfect temperature outside, not too hot or cold. I leaned up on the railing of the porch and so did Micheal. His body facing me. We started talking about the most random stuff, but it felt so natural. The conversation just went on and it was actually fun but I needed to see how late it was.

"I'm a little thirsty, I'm gonna go grab some water from the fridge. Do you want one?" I said with a dry mouth.

"Yeah, but I'll go get them, don't worry." Micheal said with a small smirk. I watched as he walked into the house, closing the door behind him. He was taking quite a long time just to get some water. I went to go inside to check on him but as soon as I went to grab the door handle. He opened the door and came out with the waters.

"Oh, thanks Micheal," I said with confusion in my voice.

"No problem, drink up," Micheal said.

I grabbed the water and quickly gulped it down. I hadn't really drank much water all day so that was refreshing. I swallowed the last bit of my water, then looked up to see Micheal looking at me with a small smirk.

"What?" I said with a small chuckle.

"Nothing, you're just cute. How about we go for a quick drive," said Micheal

"Umm sure, that could be fun," I said hesitantly.

"Okay here, the car is unlocked," Micheal said.

There was the sound of his car keys clicking as the car unlocked and we walked over. He opened the passenger side door and directed me in. He closed the door and made his way to the driver's seat. He started the car then looked over at me.

"Ready to go?" he asked.

"Yep," I said quickly.

We reversed out of the driveway and quickly drove down the road. We started taking lots of lefts and rights and we were soon very far off from my neighborhood. We were driving for a good 30 minutes before I broke the silence.

"I thought this was going to be a quick drive," I said

"Oh yeah right, we're gonna make a quick stop then we can head back," he said in his very deep voice.

I didn't respond. I couldn't read his emotions because it was so dark in the car. But it was weird. There was tension, but not the good tension. Something felt off.

"Could we actually just turn back now I'm not really feeling that good?" I asked.

"No, the stop will be quick I promise."

Before I could tell him we needed to go back I felt my eyes starting to shut and I couldn't get any words out of my mouth. Then everything went black.

Claire was knocked out cold. Micheal looked over at her

and noticed. A small grin appeared on his face as he realized the pill he put in her water worked. He drove for another 15 minutes before he pulled into a dark alleyway. He got out of the car and picked up Claire's limp body. He opened a door in the alleyway with his foot and carried her into a building. He sat her on the cold concrete floor and locked her in a cell. She was surrounded by thick metal bars. No way to get out from the inside. She laid there, her body limp, and with no recollection of where she was. Micheal went to his car and came back with gloves on up to his elbow. A mask was covering his nose and mouth. He had multiple black trash bags in his left hand and a large ax in his right. Micheal grabbed the cell key from his pocket and unlocked it. He made his way into the cell with Claire and sat the bags and ax down. He then rolled Claire's limp body over and spread her limbs out. He reached behind him and grabbed the ax with both hands and began to chop. After he finished the job, he put her body into multiple bags, threw them in the back of his car and drove away.

On the other side of the state were Claire's parents. Sleeping peacefully not knowing what happened to their only daughter. Claire's mom awoke from a dream startled in a hotel bed. She sat straight up letting out a loud gasp. She had a dream that when they got home Claire was gone so she felt like something was wrong. She woke up her husband and they decided to head home just to check on Claire and to feel better since they could not get a hold of her on the phone. They pulled into the driveway and Claire's mom quickly got out and walked to the front door, but then she stopped. She paused and picked up the black bag that was sitting on the porch in front of the door. She opened the bag, confused on why it was on the porch. A few seconds later, she let out a scream that echoed through the whole neighborhood. She was traumatized by what she saw in the bag.

A KNIGHT AT THE CROSSROADS

WESLEY PERKINSON

Inspired by Victor Vasnetsov's painting "A Knight at the Crossroads"

As the knight, seated upon his snow-white horse, stared solemnly at the headstone in front of him, the grave of the only man he ever truly understood, he reminisced on all the moments that brought him to this place.

"Today, we start our march to Baghdad!" The Khan rallied his 150,000 troops, commanding them with an iron fist in his knee-length coat. "Today, we will break Islam!" As he said this, a hundred thousand cries filled the air with an ear-piercing, soul-splitting sound that would have been heard for miles. Surrounded by troops sparring and practicing with their swords and spears, the knight remains calm. Nothing but the heat stricken desert surrounds the army. The dry, hostile environment mirroring the violent nature of the Mongolian army. With the sun beating down on the army, the knight sits alone in a yurt, sharpening his spear, reminiscing on his past, remembering the reason he's sitting in this heavy armor, the reason that he made himself a weapon of death, the one reason he fights today.

"Discipline! You may have perfect technique, you may have complete control over your weapon, but without control over your *emotions*, you will never be able to defeat your enemy."

The knight's father, also a knight within the Mongol empire, teaches his son each day to become a master of the spear. The knight's ochre complexion glowed in the evening sunlight, sweat slowly falling down his brow, his dark brown close-cropped hair gleaming from the sweat, leaning on his wooden stick which mimics a true Mongol spear. The knight, who at this time is 9 years old, admires how his father masterfully wields his weapon, puncturing and mutilating the straw dummy outside of the small hut in which they and his mother live. "Alright, son, you've done well today. Now, we will go inside and eat."

"But father! I want to keep training!" the knight complained.

"Rest, my son. A warrior is only as good as the rest which he gives himself. This, you must remember." The knight's father spoke softly but with finality.

"Fine, father." The knight sighed but complied and slowly walked into the hut, in stride with his father. Although the knight did not "We are quickly approaching Baghdad! Ready yourselves! Steady your mind! Prepare for conquest!" The collective cries of 100,000 men filled the air, and it seemed as if time stopped around the army as if everything else in the air had frozen in time, and the only thing left in the world was the army, and the target. Marching through the desert, walking under the cover of the night, the sand beating into the backs of the army, the humidity in the air causing everyone to sweat underneath their armor. In the chaos of the march, tens of thousands of men going psycho, gearing up to conquer the world, the knight walks alone. He walks, trying to gain peace, embodying the calm before the storm. He knew he could join the march with the others, or the chants and the shouts, but he knew if he wanted to be ready for this siege, he should remain calm, and stay locked in with his emotions. He knew if he wished to succeed, he needed to stay focused on his reason.

"Father! Father, no! Please!" The knight, only 2 days after he trained with his father, imagining the rest of his life with him, is now sitting at the foot of his father's grave, tears flowing like waterfalls, feeling destroyed.

"Come, young one." The knight's mother tries to console the young knight, but he refuses to move. the knight will never move from this spot. The knight will spend the rest of his life here, remembering his father, and imagining what could have been. He would never know how his father died, he just knew that one moment he was sitting in his hut with his mother, and the next moment, two Mongol soldiers were at his door, giving him the news that his father had passed away in battle. After visiting his father's grave, the young knight knew he needed to carry on his father's legacy, and from that moment he trained rigorously with his spear, taking himself to the point of exhaustion every single day, doing this all for his father.

"We are one mile out! Everyone, prepare your weapons! Prepare your minds! Prepare for destruction!" The uproar of the army could be heard from the farthest reaches of Baghdad and would have put fear into the strongest warrior. The knight, as always, walks alone, and does nothing but prepare. He did not plan on communicating with anyone in his army and imagined he would simply fight, kill, and return home.

"Hello." A man whom the knight had never seen approached him. The knight was caught off guard and quickly observed the man. He was a little over 6 foot tall, judging by the fact that the knight was slightly below eye line with this man. He seemed less muscular than the knight, with longer, less kept hair, in contrast to the knight's close-cropped hair. They had very similar skin tones, which did not surprise the knight as most people in the Mongol army came from Mongolia. Initially, the knight did not respond to this man, as he still had no intention of making simple small talk before a battle of this magnitude. He viewed conversation and relationships as futile and believed that the only person he would ever understand was himself. "Do you have no ears? Or do you simply choose to ignore me?" The man once again pried the knight, very obviously expecting a response. The knight was taken aback and decided that this man perhaps deserved his time of day.

"You are a confident man, coming up to me as you did," the knight says with a mix of admiration and annoyance.

"I have no reason not to be confident, do I? I *am* the greatest swordsman in this army, and have no reason to fear you!" The man replies in a tone bordering on cocky.

This caught the knight's attention, as he had been a part of this army for a long time, and had heard no such stories of a 'greatest swordsman'. So, whether out of curiosity, or admiration, the knight would never know, he decided to march the rest of the way with this strange man. As they arrived upon the final steps before reaching Baghdad, the knight and the man, still walking in unison, having conversed about their life, their passions, and their reasons for fighting, the knight concluded this man was worthy of being considered a true knight.

"If this is my last battle, I am glad that I get to share it with you." The knight was kind in his words, but both men knew that this first meeting they had could very well be their last.

"I am also glad that I got to share it with you." After this was said, the two men went their separate ways, readied their respective weapons, and charged into battle with a cry that could wake the dead.

The ensuing siege of Baghdad began as many other pillages had for the Mongol Empire. The knights, along with the other 100,000 troops, were met by heavy resistance at the outer limits of the city. Both knight's fought with similar expertise over their weapon, but there were very noticeable differences in the way in which they fought. The knight who wields the spear had very humble confidence in the way he fought, and never attempted to move too quickly, although he could destroy his enemy as his other Mongol troops did, he rarely found a reason to. This heavily contrasts the knight who wields the sword, as he sprints around the battlefield, will trash talk his enemy as he fights, and is very gruesome and morbid in the way he fights. In each kill, the knight attempts to humiliate his opponent before he utterly destroys him. Whether with swords or spears, mutilating, slashing, and dismembering the enemy before they had even reached the outer walls. As the Mongol forces pushed forward, slashing down any enemies in their way, the knight's mind drifted. He started to wonder more about this interesting knight. Why had he approached him? Did he have other intentions? The knight decided he could not dwell on these questions, however, as the forces were nearing the homes and inner areas of the Abbasid caliphate. The knight knew that he must steady his mind, and calm his emotions, as it was now time to do what he did best.

Both knights were very obviously masters of their craft. Whether it was the pinpoint accuracy with a spear or the inhumanly precise swings of his sword, both men seemed unstoppable. The knight was able to defeat multiple soldiers at once with his sword, slashing two troops of Baghdad before they had the chance to realize what was happening. Advancing ever closer to the center of the city, pillaging homes, killing soldiers and civilians alike, no innocent was left alive, and no stone was left unturned. The knight was faced with a close call, as he had two Islamic soldiers attack him from each side. Thankfully for him, he had practiced this situation thousands of times, and perfectly positioned his spear to block the first attack while piercing the other soldier, then flipping the spear at speeds that would rival Hermes, and slashed the other soldier before he had time to react. After nearly 5 hours of destruction, the remaining number of opposing forces within Baghdad had gone from nearly 80,000 to roughly 800. Although many had tried to surrender, Mongol forces had been taught from the moment they started fighting to show no mercy. The once bustling town, full of life and color, was now more akin to the Red Sea. Everywhere you stepped was blood, bodies, and signs of complete annihilation. As the siege was reaching its close, the knights found each other from across the city and started approaching each other, weapons sheathed, ready to finish pillaging and return home.

"Good fighting out there. I never got your name, though." the knight asks the other.

"Altantsetseg. My name is Altantsetseg." the knight says as he covers his spear.

"Good name. My name is Ganbaatar. Named after my father." In this moment of weakness, the split second in which neither man had a complete understanding of their surroundings, was the time in which one of the few remaining Muslim soldiers stabbed one of the knights. The knight fell to the ground, his weapon clanging onto the floor. The other knight screamed out and slew this Muslim soldier in a moment of pure rage. Once the knight was done with this soldier, the only proof there was ever a human there was the pools of blood on the ground. The knight knelt on the ground, shook the other knight lightly, and checked for a pulse. There was no pulse. He said a quick Mongolian prayer over the body, shut his eyelids and joined the rest of the troops around the Khan.

After the fighting was over, the knight got onto his white horse, covered his spear, and started the trek to finish the journey of the one man he understood. Riding through the desert, on the back of his horse, looking like a snowflake in a sea of sand. He rode on his horse in no hurry, remembering all the moments that led to him being where he is now, all the moments that culminated in this final journey. He is almost completely bare, with nothing but the clothes he was wearing. No food, no water, nothing else but him, his horse, and his memories.

After days of riding, days of being cut off from the knights and people he had known for so long, he finally crossed out of the desert and into the plains. He knew he was approaching the resting place, and started to almost feel lighter, as if he was becoming one with the wind. He thought nothing of this, however, as he assumed he was just becoming dehydrated and hungry. He had been seated upon this white horse for nearly a week, neither of them had stopped even once. They had not stopped for food, rest, water, or anything. They simply strode through the terrain around them, sometimes seemingly going over mountains and floating across the water, but he was sure this must be hallucinations.

If the knight was being honest with himself, he wasn't sure how either he or the horse were still going at the pace they were, let alone going at all. After time stopped seeming linear, after time stopped seeming like it wasn't moving at all, by the point that time no longer existed within the knight's mind, he finally reached the end of his journey. Resting upon the top of a hill which he had no idea how he and his snow white horse reached, with patches of dead grass, and scattered rocks around the hilltop, was one single headstone placed in the center with a crow flying around it.

The closer that the knight got to the headstone, the less attached he seemed to be to the world around him. He assumed that weeks of not eating or drinking were getting to him, but this felt different. This was a feeling he had never experienced before, and words couldn't describe how his body felt. So as the knight, seated upon his snow white horse, staring solemnly at the gravestone in front of him, staring at the grave of the only person he ever understood, he read the name engraved in the stone one last time.

"Altantsetseg." As he read his name off of this gravestone, he finally understood the finality of life and death. So, seated upon his snow-white horse, he rode over the horizon, and into the unknown light.

GRAY

REAGAN POWELL

It is the only thing I've seen since being shipped out to this god forsaken war with the 83rd battalion, and the first thing I see when I awaken in my cot. While sluggishly forcing myself out of standard issue bedrolls, which were scratchy and thin, I felt all the weight of the battles that I had fought so far to get to Warsaw; where the 83rd now sat just 12 miles northeast of the city. Today was the day we took the city.

However, before that, I must get ready. I am the first of the battalion to awake at 05:56, 4 minutes before our supervisor would wake up the rest of the battalion. As I made my way to the bathroom quarters of our barracks I made sure to stay quiet so as to not awaken the other soldiers. As I quietly close the restroom door, I lean over the sink and stair into the mirror, just to see a reflection that looks like an empty shell of myself. While staring at that reflection, without opening my mouth, the reflection contorts a smile a speaks.

Good Morning Peter. The empty shell spoke to me like It was an entity separate from myself, however I knew he *was a part of me.*

"Tod," I spoke back to him. I thought personally the name fit as it was German for death. Tod, being a presence in my psyche that has manifested himself into my very being. He is a blood-thirsty spirit that haunts me and is trying to force me to give up control of my body. Ever since I was drafted I've not just heard his voice, but I've also seen visions. Things like small children running alongside our battalion, deformed wild foxes and deers just outside of full view, and voices at night, beckoning me into the dark night of the wilderness surrounding our barracks.

Today is the day you storm Warsaw right?

"Yes, it is Tod, why?" I responded.

You know you're gonna have to kill a pole right?

"Yes I do." I said annoyed.

It'll be easy for me to take control of your mind then.

"We'll see." I responded as I turned and left the restroom.

You can't escape me Peter. Was the last thing I heard before leaving the bathroom. From there his voice was quiet and I considered telling my superior, the *Feldwebel,* however I knew that if I told him the reason I didn't want to storm the city, then I would be sent to one of the several concentration camps throughout Europe. Where I would surely then be starved, beaten, tortured, and eventually killed in a mass gas chamber. I've made it this far, not giving myself up now.

As soon as I stepped out of the bathroom there was chaos, privates blaring bugles, and everyone scrambling and running to get their things together by 07:15. I however, calmly dressed myself in my *waffenrock* coat. Grabbing my rifle from the armory, I proceed towards the loading bay portion of the base and line up in roll call formation. As I am waiting for the sergeant to get here I feel a nervous feeling rise in my stomach, the feeling that Tod might actually be able to take control of my psyche. I am then snapped out of my trance by our sergeant.

"ATTENTION!" he said. Everyone immediately stood erect. He then started to list the names of the fifteen specifically selected soldiers until he got to the last one, me.

"MUELER!" He yelled.

"SIR, ATTENDING, SIR!" I respond

"Everyone load up now, we are leaving."

All the soldiers loaded up into the back of four of the many *Kubelwagen* on the base, which were similar to the American *Jeep*. I was assigned to sit with private Schidt and Private Taylor, two cousins from Munich in southern Germany, far away from where I grew up in Rostock. Schidt was a very stoic man, maybe 6 '2-6' 3, with shoulders as broad as a barn and arms the size of cannonballs. He didn't speak much, but when he did his voice was similar to a thunder clap which pierced through the air and evoked silence after it came, he also had jet black eyes, similar to the fur of a well kept lamb, silky, shiny, smooth, with a piercing gaze. Taylor however was very different from Schidt, he was a slimmer man, no heavier than 155 pounds, and only stood at 5 '8.5. He was ferocious; however, a fiery voice to go along with his calculated aggression in training and his fragrant humor. His blonde hair and blue eyes alone had earned him favor in the eyes of our direct superior, the Third Reich.

"You boys ready for a fight?" said Taylor.

"Of course I am." I responded. Schidt simply responded with a low grunt.

"Good, we are gonna be a part of the first unit," explained Taylor. "We are gonna infiltrate the city under the guise of being Polish soldiers coming to provide reinforcements to fortify the city." I nodded in agreement after he said this. Taylor then pulls out a map of the city and points to a circled building near the center.

"That right there, gentlemen, is the Prudential tower of Warsaw." said Taylor. "Mueler, it gonna be your job to go to the top of it and launch a smoke signal, that'll inform the rest of our infantry to begin invading the city."

"How do I know when to light it?" I asked.

"That's the part when the rest of our battalion comes in." Explained Taylor. "We have 6 different exits to the city that we are going to have to lock down before you launch that signal. Once that happens Schmidt will find you and tell you to launch to signal."

"Roger that, Taylor." I responded, right before seeing the city emerge over the horizon.

We're here. I dreaded the sound of his voice.

You will give yourself to me.

I refuse to listen to his voice as we drive into the entrance of the city where we are met by our enemy.

"What brings you to Warsaw today?" Says a kind lady with smooth brown hair and silky brown eyes.

"We are here to fortify the city from the invading Germans." Says Taylor.

"Come on through then." Says the woman.

We drive our way through town and eventually pull up right to the Prudential building. As we made our way through town however, I saw things. Those same children who I knew couldn't be real as they seemingly ran through people and teleported through cars, and also didn't have faces. As well as visions of a looming figure, tall, lanky, and grotesque with my face. I tried to shake off the visions but it was hard. I made my way to the entrance of the building with Schidt behind me. In a lumbering voice he said.

"I'll create a distraction while you find your way to the roof from inside, once you're ready wait till you hear the truck horn sound 3 times, then launch the signal."

"Roger that." I responded.

Schidt then proceeded to slam open the doors of the building and yelled.

"Invasion! Invasion! The Germans have arrived!" As everyone then proceeded to yell and scream as they fled from the building.

"Hurry, we're now on a time crunch but we have the

perfect distraction. Start the signal by 08:08 no matter what. Go!" Schidt stopped me and said.

I made my way through the building swiftly and discreetly. Going up the building was no simple task as there were thousands of civilians, but I made it work. After approximately 13 minutes I had made my way to the roof. *08:01.* I quickly manned the signal and it was ready to fire as I looked up and saw it.

Hello, Old friend. The figure that stood there was more terrifying than any monster or mythical creature, it was me. Immediately, I knew what I had to do, I drew my standard issue Walther p-38 pistol and took aim.

You wouldn't dare!

"Oh yes I would." I finalized. As I pulled the trigger in order in fleeting hope of finally killing the thing that had been tormenting me since the loss of my mother to polish combat. But then it all snapped.

"Wh-w-why, Meuler?" said Taylor as he stood their, blood coming from his abdomen. He however quickly came to and pounced on me, strangling and thrashing at my neck until my consciousness faded, the last thing I was able to make out was the muffled screams of Taylor and Schidt as I faded away.

And that brings us to where I am now. I'm writing this document from a Polish prison cell in Lubin, I was abandoned by Schidt but something tells me the private Taylor still hasn't left Warsaw. I've felt free these past few days sitting in this cell, not once have I felt any unease, had any visions, or heard voices. I believe that getting private Taylors blood on my hands has released me from my suffering in a way, sort of like a messed up baptism. But, it doesn't matter now, because as a German POW in Poland, I am now awaiting my death sentence.

Oh wait, there the officers are, calling for me now. So just as I gave Taylor the taste of death, I wonder if I as well will now be meeting the same fate

LOVE AT FIRST SIGHT

TAYLEE READING

Inspired by M.C. Escher's painting "Twon Tree"

His hair fell perfectly above his ears as though it was never even touched. His curls fell in his face hiding parts of his eyes. He was tall, slightly muscular and had the face of a Greek god. He looked perfect. James was everything I wanted and more. As a 16 year old girl, it was completely normal to find someone attractive, but he wasn't just attractive, he was kind. He treated everyone with respect, even me. Although he and I haven't spoken all that much, I can tell he has a good heart. He's so caring that it's almost weird. Like he cares too much about everything, in a good way of course.

He's so perfect. I was so surprised when he asked me out I almost laughed, cried, and threw up all at once, but I didn't. Instead, all that came out was a small squeak and a head nod. He looked at me funny at first and then smiled. He set a date for us to meet up to which I nodded my head again and then he walked away. It seemed unreal, like I was in a dream or something. I'm still embarrassed at my reaction.

“Hey Evelyn!” I looked up to see James running towards me with his hand raised as if to wave down a taxi. He slowed to a jog and finally to a walk when he got right next to me and my locker. “Are we still on for Friday?” he asked as my face turned a bright red. I could feel the heat in my cheeks and ears.

“Yeah, of course,” I said looking down at my shoes trying not to make eye contact with the beautiful man standing in front of me.

“Good! I'll see you then. Six, remember?” He almost sounded worried I wouldn't come

“Yeah, okay. See you then!” I replied.

I watched him jog away to class. He was always jogging. He nearly fell into a wall and then turned the corner. I smiled at myself. I had been obsessed with him ever since 6th grade but he never seemed to notice me until now. I walked into class as the bell rang and sat next to Mia and Ava. Mia had short, light brown curly hair. She had rectangular glasses that sat perfectly on the bridge of her nose and beautiful hazel green eyes. Ava on the other hand had long, straight black hair. She wore a lot of eyeliner and lipstick. They were equally beautiful, just in different ways.

"Are you excited for your date tomorrow?" Ava asked.

"Yeah, I am. I'm just also really nervous," I replied.

"Don't worry, you'll be fine." Mia chimed in.

"Yeah, I hope so," I said almost to myself, looking at my shoes under the desk.

A few hours passed and I was at home. The days seem to go by faster and faster the older I get. I like to sit on my bed and look around my room. My room is my favorite place in the house. My room is my own space, my shell that I can sit in and not do anything. I look around to my lavender walls and try to trace my eyes around every corner of my room. The stuffed animals were still in their designated place and my books were on my bookshelf in the right corner of my room. My clothes were still folded on top of my dresser from the night before when I forgot to put them away. It makes me feel good knowing that my room is my very own space. My childhood was amazing. I saw everything in bright colors and through rose colored glasses. My parents were never abusive in any way and always treated me as their equal. That's most likely because they had a lot of issues trying to have a child. I am an only child and they said that that was all they needed. My childhood was very good compared to most. I was spoiled and treated kindly but I was still raised to be humble and kind.

I lay down on my cream white bed and look up at my ceiling. I try to make faces in the weird shapes I see. My eyes start to feel heavy and soon enough I fall asleep. The next morning felt unreal. It was the day I was going on my date. I dressed up nice for school that day with my favorite pair of baggy jeans and a tight tank top. I put on a little bit of blush and mascara and left the house. The entire school day I was trying to look nice. And then I was home. I took a shower, put on a cute casual dress, and touched up my makeup and hair.

"Evelyn honey, James is here!" My mom yelled from downstairs.

"Coming!" I said as I looked at myself one last time

I ran down the stairs to meet with a man dressed in a nice expensive suit. He was barely recognizable. "James?" I asked.

"Yeah, that's me," he said while giggling at my question.

"Ok, bye mom, I love you," I said as I walked out of the door.

I got into James's truck and buckled my seat belt. He started to drive away from my house and I suddenly felt sick.

"So, where are we going?" I asked trying not to throw up

"It's a surprise," he said as he turned onto some wooded back roads. The way he said it made my skin crawl. I so desperately wanted to go back home, but I stayed silent. I thought that if I pretended to be cool that he would like me more and I knew for a fact that if I said I wanted to go home he would rightfully get upset. Soon enough we reached a clearing in the middle of nowhere. Just a blank spot in the middle of the woods, surrounded by trees. It looked like an unfinished painting. He got out of the car and grabbed something from the back of his truck. I tried to look back to see what he was doing but it was so dark I was basically blind. All of a sudden he opened the passenger door and helped me out of the truck. Whatever he had grabbed he had obviously hidden behind his back.

"Do you trust me, Evelyn?" he asked as though he was about to cry

"Uh- yeah...yeah of course I do," I replied with hesitation.

"Good. Then you'll be quiet," he said calmly.

"What-" I tried to speak but was cut off.

A bag went over my head and my hands were behind my back before I knew it. "No, wait! I want to go home now! James!" I tried to scream but the bag muffled all of my words.

"Shhh, you said you trusted me," he said as though he were my father trying to comfort me. He started to push me around and we started walking straight into the woods. All I could think about was how I was going to die. I was so young and haven't lived my life yet. My poor parents wouldn't know what to do. I didn't want to die yet. My thoughts ran through my head so fast I hadn't realized we had come to a stop. He shoved me one last time and I fell onto a wooden floor. He ripped the bag off of my head and angrily told me to get up. I scrambled up to my feet as best as I could with my hands behind my back. He grabbed my arms and walked me to a set of stairs. There was a dark wooden door right next to the stairs with a gold door knob and a green curtain covering a hole. He shoved me up the stairs and I looked around for any details I could. We were in a cabin, a very large one at that.

When we reached the top of the stairs he walked me to a room with a pink bed and a small white desk with some books in the corner. The curtains were sheer white. There was a small white bunny on the bed with a notebook and pen.

"Why are we here?" I tried to ask with my shaky voice.

"Don't ask questions," James replied with an angry tone. He untied my hands and tried to force off my dress.

"No!" I screamed so loud my ears rang. Soon my face was met with such a hard slap that I froze. He continued to force off my dress and tears rolled down my eyes. However, to my surprise, he put a pale pink sweater on me and a pair of white sweat pants. He grabbed me again and took me downstairs. He stopped at the door right next to the stairs and took out a skeleton key to unlock it. The door slowly creaked open into a pit of darkness.

"Come with me, don't make a sound," he said as if he were waiting for something to happen. I slowly walked down the stairs behind him. I stepped lightly, ready to run the other direction if I needed to. Soon I got to the bottom of the stairs and James had already turned on the lights and stood in front of a large white curtain. He faced the curtain, shaking.

"What's going on? Why am I here? What's the point of all of this?" I asked, getting more and more scared as time went on.

"Stay still, I don't want this to get any worse than it is," he said, still facing the curtain.

"What do you mean-" My sentence was cut off from him ripping the curtain to the side. Behind the curtain was a gruesome rotting corpse that was still moving. Its teeth were black and its tongue was a dark crimson red. I ran up the stairs and closed the door to the basement behind me. I ran out of the cabin hearing James screaming, pleading for his life. I shut my eyes as the adrenaline ran through my veins. I kept running until I couldn't run any longer. I untied my hands from behind which was no easy task. I threw the rope on the ground and sat down. The dirt felt cool with the night air, the trees blew in the wind as I sat with my thoughts.

I thought about everything that happened in the span of twenty minutes. I was kidnapped, changed, shoved in a basement with a zombie and was going to be fed to it. I heard screams from afar. I rushed away from where I was sitting trying to find my way through the trees. Rain started to pour and the pink sweater was becoming increasingly more soaked. The sweater would latch onto every tree branch possible as I ran through the woods, Mud all over my pants and shoes. I ran and I ran and I ran until I got to the clearing again. I followed the truck marks out of the woods and walked home. Three days later the end of the world began. People rose from the dead to simply terrorize others. I'm starting to think that this was my fault for leaving the front door of the cabin open.

THE BALLERINA IN WHITE

MILEY ROBERTS

An extremely chilly day had arrived in a small American city. The night sky was dimmed by the presence of snow-filled clouds. Snowflakes were carried by the cold wind as they swept through the city's streets. What had once been green grass lay beneath blankets of snow, as snowflakes continued to glide gently across the area. The trees were without leaves, but they had lovely icicles hanging from their dormant branches.

The sun started to emerge as it slowly began rising. As the sun's rays broke through the clouds above. The dark city was soon filled with light. The snow on the ground began to shimmer. Within a few hours of the sun rising, the area quickly changed from being quiet to shockingly busy. People could be heard conversing while cars were idling and songbirds were chirping.

However, a little deeper into the city was the home of Madison May, where our story truly begins. Madison's eyes opened to the grating shrieks of her alarm clock as the sun's light crept through her bedroom window. She yawned, sat up, and turned off her alarm clock. After a brief stretch, she smiled when she saw the snow falling outside. Her mother always loved the snow so, naturally, she did too. While Madison made her way downstairs she could hear the delicious sounds of bacon sizzling in the kitchen.

Once Madison made it downstairs she entered the kitchen and saw her mother preparing breakfast and her father waiting at the dining room table. Apart from the sizzles of cooking and the clanging of cooking utensils, there was only silence. But taking into account that everyone had just woken up, this was normal. Madison entered the dining room and took a seat at the table to wait. Still, no one spoke for a few minutes. The silence persisted until Madison's dad spoke up.

“Good morning, Madison,” he said with a loving smile on his face as he looked at Madison.

“Morning dad,” Madison replied as she turned her head to look at him, and returned the loving smile.

The brief greeting came to an abrupt end when Olivia’s mother handed plates to them. Some eggs and bacon were neatly arranged on the plates, hot and fresh. Madison and her father started eating without any hesitation. After a few moments he realized that his wife had not joined him and Madison at the table for breakfast. He placed his knife and fork on the table and gave her a quick look. He prepared to speak. Madison noticed this and her head perked up to listen to what he had to say.

"Olivia, dear, are you going to eat?" he asked her with an arched eyebrow.

"I'm not hungry this morning, Nicholas. I'll eat later," Olivia replied as she looked at Nicholas with a reassuring smile.

"If you say so," Nicholas said as he turned back to his plate of food. He continued to eat, but a lot slower than before.

Olivia silently fled upstairs. When he heard Olivia go, Nicholas couldn't help but sigh. With hesitation, he now just stared at his meal. Without her present, he felt odd sitting down to eat. Following that, he moved his plate back and got up from his chair. He left the dining room and made his way upstairs. Madison was left alone at the table with her meal.

Madison scowled as she lost her appetite. What purpose did eating breakfast serve anyway? Lunch is always available. She got up and cleared her plate because she had to leave for school soon anyway. She put the plate away and went upstairs to her room to get ready. After about ten minutes, she was prepared to leave. She didn't really care about her appearance or what she wore to school.

Why dress up when she had dance after school, anyway? It would simply take more time to get out of. It was fortunate that she didn't take too long to get ready because the bus had already arrived. Though she was about to speak, Madison refrained. In any case, her parents were probably preoccupied with adult topics. Silently, she stepped outside and onto the bus. She plugged in her headphones and started listening to music as soon as she boarded the bus. Her forgetting about this morning might be eased by doing that.

The bus had left, and the start of the school day was approaching. Madison sat motionless, mouthing the song she was listening to as she gazed out the window. The bus was at the high school in no time. Everyone, including Madison, started to dismount the bus and enter the high school. In order to wait for the bell to ring so that first period could begin, she went to the gym.

The bell rang after a short while, and Madison got up to go to her first period class even though she knew it would be a long day. Madison simply did her own thing all day. Working and paying attention to lectures. Honestly, she felt like nothing interesting was happening throughout the day. It was just another dull school day. Despite the "cool kids" funny but stupid antics, it was still pretty boring. After enduring it for seven hours, Madison was completely exhausted.

Thankfully though, the day was finally over, allowing Madison to head to her favorite place, her dance studio. She would hopefully be able to take part in competitions. She gathered her belongings, left the high school, and headed for the dance studio. It was only a few blocks away.

She arrived, and when she saw the other dancers and the dance instructor, a huge smile appeared on her face. As soon as she had put her belongings down, she went to change into her dance attire. When she was prepared, she went to the designated spot. She cast a quick glance around, spotting some unfamiliar faces. She questioned whether they were her competition. The recognizable faces waved at Madison, and it appeared that they had distracted her. She waved back with joy, but then the dance instructor suddenly made a loud clearing of her throat. Everyone went silent.

"Ladies, as most of you know, we're a ballet dance studio. We compete against each other during dance competitions for pricey rewards thanks to our sponsors," the dance instructor said loudly, her voice a bit raspy. "All of you will be learning individual dances to assigned songs for a dance competition in two weeks! So, make sure you work hard and pay attention," she continued glancing at everyone on the floor.

The dance instructor appeared to have finished speaking; she nodded and departed to make notes for this dance lesson. Madison was approached by a number of girls she recognized from prior events. Madison and the girls engaged in brief conversation while grinning and laughing. The dance instructor wasn't gone long before she was back with the lesson prepared. As the lesson began, everyone returned to their positions and paid close attention. From the splits, to flips, then twirls, all the girls followed instruction to the best of their abilities.

Madison was even more worn out than before after two hours had passed. She was, however, very eager for the competition in two weeks. It was time to leave for home. Madison questioned who would be picking her up. She walked out of the dance studio and hopped into her parent's car. Today, she had been picked up by her mother, Olivia. Madison grinned and was about to say something. However, when she caught sight of her mother, who was strangely pale, she said nothing. She frowned worriedly in silence. She didn't want to say anything until they got home.

They drove home in awkward silence. Both got out of the car and entered the house. No matter how much she wanted to, Madison was hesitant to speak. Even though all she wanted to do was ask her mother a question, she didn't want her mother to worry. She held back for a moment before speaking after some internal deliberation.

"Hey mom? Are you feeling alright?" Madison asked in a gentle, but anxious tone of voice.

Olivia was hesitant to respond for a moment, before replying in a newfound raspy voice. "I'm fine sweetheart, don't worry. I'm just a little tired is all."

Madison gave a brief nod, but she didn't believe it. Her mother sounded horribly ill in her hoarse voice. She considered bringing up the subject, but decided against it since Olivia did indeed appear to be exhausted. She went to her room, leaving Olivia alone while keeping her thoughts to herself. She had homework to do anyway. She gently shut the door after entering her room. Her next move was to sit down at her desk and try to forget everything for now. In order to start working on her homework, she looked through her backpack for the assignments. Her father's voice could be heard from downstairs after she had been working on homework for a while.

"Madison! Come downstairs! It's dinner time!" Nicholas said loudly. Madison closed her notebook, "Coming!" she replied with the same volume.

Madison had, fortunately, completed her homework just in time. She gathered all of her paperwork and put it in her backpack. After completing that, she got to her feet and went downstairs to the dining room. As soon as she entered the dining room, she saw her parents seated at the table with plates of food in front of them. Dinner was some nicely arranged spaghetti, and she sat down in front of her plate in silence. She started to eat alongside her parents. Nothing was said. However, after a short while, Olivia started to cough. She even sounded like she was having trouble breathing due to her rough coughing. Although she had given up smoking, her cough was worse compared to when she did. She hurriedly got up from the table and entered another room while still violently coughing. Madison and Nicholas exchanged a worried look as Nicholas quickly got up to follow Olivia, leaving Madison by herself at the table.

Madison felt sick to her stomach at the sound of Olivia coughing, which also made her lose her appetite. She stood up, threw her plate in the trash, and went to her room. To be well-rested for tomorrow's school day, she made the decision to simply go to bed.

In the blink of an eye, two weeks had passed. Olivia's

condition had not changed, and the school days had been monotonous as usual. However, tonight was the night of Madison's first dance competition of the year. As she ate her lunch quietly, she was incredibly happy and eager for the school day to be over. She noticed herself daydreaming throughout lunch and her subsequent classes about the competition tonight. Which made time pass even more quickly. The school day had already ended before she realized it.

Madison walked out of the school and heard the rumbling of the bus. To prepare for tonight, she boarded the bus and headed home. The bus had finally arrived at her house after much impatient waiting. She hurried inside after getting off the bus to prepare for tonight's events. Her dancing was inspired by a sad song, and she wore a tutu that was a decent length and a dark shade of blue along with the rest of it.

She sprinted down the stairs grinning broadly. As Madison awaited them downstairs, Olivia and Nicholas were already there. As their daughter hurried out of the house and into the car, her parents grinned at her. Behind her, the two followed. After everyone got in the car, they departed for the dance studio.

By the time they got out of the car and into the studio, they noticed that they had arrived early. While Madison made her way backstage to get ready, Olivia and Nicholas took their seats in the auditorium facing the stage. More spectators quickly filled the auditorium, and more dancers began to arrive behind the stage. Within a few minutes, the seats were filled with a decently sized crowd, and all the dancers were stretching back-stage. Two girls Madison recognized from last year, Chloe and Lila, walked up to her as she was stretching. Chloe was the first to speak as both girls grinned at Madison.

"Good luck, Madison! I'm sure you'll do great!" Chloe said sweetly with a cheeky smile. Madison smiled at Chloe.

"Thank you! I wish you both the best of luck as well!" she replied with an upbeat and joyful voice. Lila simply nodded timidly without speaking. Chloe grinned as she and Lila walked off to another location to stretch. Madison grinned quietly. As the competition started, the lights started to dim. The stage was lit beautifully. The first contestant stood up and performed a graceful entrance dance. As she waited for her turn, Madison watched in awe.

Numerous dancers completed their dances one after the other until Madison's turn came. She closed her eyes and concentrated solely on the music and her dance. She gracefully moved to the tune of the somber song that was assigned to her. Up until the shouts from a recognizable voice came from the crowd, everything was going well for her. Madison's song came to an abrupt end, and she stood there and listened.

"CALL 9-1-1!" Nicholas shouted in a panic as he held Olivia's unconscious body.

Madison froze in shock when she realized what was happening and saw her mother lying motionless in her father's arms. Madison was paralyzed and just stood there as people frantically dialed 9-1-1. Olivia was quickly transported in an ambulance after it arrived moments after. Nicholas rushed to the car while feeling incredibly stressed. Madison ran after him in a panic.

The two jumped in the car and drove quickly alongside the ambulance. This was all happening so fast. Madison's eyes were fixated on the ambulance carrying her mother, making it difficult for her to think clearly. They arrived at the hospital quickly. While Olivia was being transported to the emergency room by the doctors, Nicholas and Madison quickly exited the vehicle to follow.

Madison's mind was swimming with thoughts and feelings all at once. As she moved quickly next to her unconscious mother and the doctors, she felt as though a powerful tsunami of emotions had just suddenly hit her in the heart. Even though she wanted to cry, she was unable to do so. The conflicting nature of all these feelings added to the stress. But she had to ignore it and concentrate on Olivia.

The doctors began their work as soon as Olivia entered the emergency room, but Nicholas and Madison were forced to wait outside. It was awful, they both found it difficult to wait for hours on end in the hospital, just hoping Olivia would be okay.

Four hours later, thankfully, a doctor finally approached them to inform them of everything. As they anticipated what the doctor would say, Nicholas and Madison's heads perked up.

"Are you two the family of Olivia May?" the doctor asked while holding a clipboard.

Nicholas quickly nodded. "Yes, we are. How is she? Is she okay?" he replied quickly, extremely worried and distressed. Madison silently listened.

"She's stabilized for the most part, but we would like to keep her for a week or two to run some tests on her. Visitations are allowed during this time," the doctor said. She then wrote something down on the clipboard she was holding.

Nicholas sighed in relief, and then he slowly nodded. "Okay, thank you," he said as he fiddled with his thumbs.

The doctor nodded before quickly leaving for an unknown location. Madison silently absorbed this knowledge before finally releasing her tense shoulders. She had a sense of optimism. Nicholas signaled for Madison to follow him back to the car because he knew they couldn't stay at the hospital any longer. Quickly recognizing this, Madison stood up and followed him.

They moved toward the car without exchanging any words. Both of them were thinking so much at once that they chose not to communicate as they entered the vehicle. The drive home was very quiet and tense. There was no denying that both of them had a difficult evening. They arrived at their house, got out of the car, and entered. Being at home without Olivia made them both feel as though something was missing. They split up after entering and went to their rooms. With a sigh, Madison quietly closed the door behind her. She didn't see the point in staying up to eat dinner, so she just went to bed. She didn't feel hungry anyway.

It was awful how Olivia's absence increased from a few days to two weeks. Even though the doctor said they wanted to keep her for that long, Madison was hopeful she would've been back sooner. Madison experienced a sense of emptiness throughout the house and a void in her heart. But thankfully, it was the weekend at the moment, so school wasn't going to add on to the stress. As soon as she heard her father's voice, she left her room and went downstairs with curiosity. He seemed to be talking on the phone.

"Okay. Thank you," she heard Nicholas say with a sorrowful tone. He hung up the phone and immediately noticed Madison.

"Madison, come here, we need to talk." He said as he pointed to the living room couch. He sat down, waiting for Madison to follow suit.

"Okay, who were you on the phone with?" Madison asked as she sat down next to him on the couch. She looked at him while waiting patiently for him to reply.

He inhaled deeply, trying not to cry in front of his clueless daughter. However his efforts lead to no avail. He turned to look at Madison as tears started to well up in his eyes. He was unable to express what needed to be said. Madison waited quietly and with patience. She knew well enough that it had to hurt if it was painful enough to make her father cry.

Nicholas needed a few seconds to collect himself before he could speak. He inhaled deeply and wiped the tears from his eyes. He noticed a steady decrease in heart rate and a return to a regular breathing cycle. The living room was silent, but that hadn't been unusual lately. Finally, he turned back towards Madison and spoke.

"No father should have to explain this to their child, but your mother was diagnosed with stage three lung cancer. Her prior smoking, according to them, was the root of the problem. I've spent all the extra money on current treatments, but without her earning an income, there won't be any extra money for additional care. I only make enough to cover the bills, purchase essentials, and other expenses." He explained thoroughly, his voice just filled with heartbreak and sadness. His eyes began to burn with tears again as he wiped them away swiftly.

Within seconds of taking everything in, Madison's eyes widened and tears began to fall down her face. She cried out inconsolably while covering her face with her hands. She had no desire to accept what she had been told. Despite how much she wanted to deny it, her dad's sobbing showed that it was all true. Nicholas frowned and gave Madison a tender hug. He intended to offer her some solace and possibly obtain some comfort himself. They hugged for a while and then released each other. Madison couldn't speak at this time. She was just rendered speechless by the news about her mother. Tears still streamed down her face. Without saying anything, she got up and went upstairs to her room, leaving Nicholas alone in the living room. She closed the door behind her and immediately laid down in bed. She wrapped a blanket around herself tightly, then silently sobbed to herself. She cried in silence for thirty minutes before falling asleep.

Nicholas got up early the following morning. He got up from the couch and walked upstairs. He was now standing in front of Madison's bedroom door. After knocking on her door and getting no answer, he slowly opened the door. Madison was still silently asleep. Without a moment to waste, he gently shook Madison awake.

"Hey, we're visiting Olivia at the hospital in a bit. Please get ready," he said with a monotone voice as he then left the room, closing the door behind him.

While getting out of bed and heading to her closet to grab some clothes to change into, Madison sighed. Even though she adored her mother, she didn't want to see her in this condition. She didn't have much of a choice, though. After some time, Nicholas was downstairs and ready, waiting for Madison. After she arrived downstairs, they both silently walked to the car and started their drive. The ride to the hospital was a bit tense, but was tolerable. It didn't take them long to arrive at the hospital. After getting out of the vehicle, they both entered the building. As she assumed he knew where to go, Madison was now just following behind Nicholas.

They eventually arrived at the room where Olivia was being held after trudging down excruciatingly long hallways and using an extremely crowded elevator. After a brief moment of hesitation, Nicholas knocked on the door and entered the room, followed by Madison. When Nicholas saw Olivia in such bad shape, he couldn't help but cry. She was attached to numerous machines, her skin was pale, and she had lost a few pounds. He simply left the room and stood outside while sobbing uncontrollably. Seeing her in that state was too much for him to bear. Madison was simply crying away in the background, trembling slightly as she stood there. However, Olivia was awake and witnessed everything. She looked at Madison with a feeble head turn. Her face lit up with a smile.

"Come here dear," Olivia said. Her voice was soft, and barely audible. However, Madison heard her and slowly walked closer, she was now standing right next to Olivia. "Don't worry about me, just keep dancing and be yourself," her mother said with a smile on her face.

Madison's face was covered in tears as she only nodded. She was currently unable to speak. She was able to witness the immense suffering her mother was experiencing just by looking at her. That upset her to the core. Nicholas suddenly returned and motioned for Madison to come on as soon as he was in the room. While waving her mother off, Madison only nodded. After seeing Olivia in that condition, they both appeared completely scarred as they left the hospital. Madison went right to her room when they got home. She started contemplating what her mother had said. Her eyes widened as an idea suddenly came to her. She quickly exited her room, hurried downstairs, and entered the living room. Where Nicholas was sitting on the couch watching tv.

"Dad! I have an idea!" She exclaimed with a huge smile on her face. Nicholas paused the TV and turned to Madison with an arched eyebrow. "An idea about what?"

"You said you don't make enough income to pay for mom's treatments, so what if I just work really hard at dance competitions and use the winning money for her treatments?" Madison asked.

Nicholas's eyes widened. He had never thought about that. He took a second to add up everything financially in his head before looking back at Madison was a huge smile.

"That could actually work! But, are you sure you want to do that?" He asked, a bit skeptical.

Madison immediately nodded. "If it'll help mom, then yes," She replied with a determined look on her face. Nicholas nodded in response. Before he could say anything else Madison was already back up in her room, finding ways to practice her future dances. She experienced a brand-new kind of tenacity that she had never experienced before, but it was motivating. Without a moment to waste she got to work.

After a brief period of time, her next dance competition was approaching. She had been practicing her dance moves nonstop in her room for the previous few days. As her father took her to the dance studio, she sat in silence, a fierce look of determination on her face. When they arrived, Nicholas sat down in a seat and Madison hurried to the backstage area to stretch. While doing so, she kept a safe distance from the other dancers. Each dancer completed their dances one at a time. Madison entered the stage once it was her turn to dance. She got into position, closed her eyes, and started to move gracefully to the music. She concentrated entirely while dancing, only thinking about her mother. She exited the stage after her performance while anxiously awaiting the result.

The name Madison May appeared next to the symbol for first place after the judges had made their choice. Madison could not help but jump up and down and cheer. After much applause, joy, and receiving the cash prize. Madison and her father departed from the studio on their way home. Nicholas drove with so much happiness.

"You did it! Madi, this is amazing! What do you plan on doing when you get home? I bet you're exhausted after that!" Nicholas said happily.

"I plan on practicing for the next competition," Madison replied with a sudden monotone voice as she glanced out her window.

That caught Nicholas off guard. "Oh, uh, are you sure? You know you have two weeks until the next one, right?" he asked with a hint of worry in his tone.

"I'm aware, but if I want to keep mom alive with these treatments, then I need to work harder." Madison said with narrowed eyes. Nicholas didn't say anything else after that. He thought that if he pressed the issue, it would only stress her out. He knew she was already overly stressed. He couldn't help but worry a bit about her, though. And he was appreciative of her determination and commitment. After thinking a little too much they had reached their house.

Madison went right to her room. With some unease in his thoughts, Nicholas watched her.

After a few days, Nicholas noticed that Madison's only activity was attending school and then practicing dance moves in her room. He took action because it was a pretty predictable cycle. He walked in front of Madison's door and knocked.

"Yeah?" Madison replied through the door.

Nicholas cleared his throat, "Hey! You've been working extra hard these past few days! Do you want to go visit your mom with me and take a break?" He asked as he just stood there.

"I can't right now! Maybe next time!" Madison replied as she continued to practice her dancing.

When Nicholas heard Madison's response, his eyes grew wide. He didn't anticipate her declining the opportunity to see her mother. He sighed and went downstairs to get his coat before leaving for the hospital. Meanwhile, Madison stuck to practicing her dances and avoiding doing anything else for the next two weeks. Her only goal was to win every dance competition she possibly could. She was already warming up alone backstage for her upcoming dance competition today. Chloe and Lila, however, suddenly came over to Madison and smiled at her as they always do.

"Hey Madison! Congratulations on winning the last competition! I wish you luck today!" Lila exclaimed happily.

"Me, too!" Chloe added with a huge grin.

"I won't need it," Madison said boldly. "I'd advise you

both to stay out of my way. I have more important things to worry about," she said firmly as she glared at Chloe and Lila.

Lila and Chloe both had startled and terrified expressions on their faces. They made a frowning exit as they moved slowly. Only rolling her eyes, Madison kept on stretching. The competition began shortly after that. With a disgusted expression on her face, Madison observed the other dancers as they performed. She didn't see them as anything more than obstacles to her efforts to save her mother's life.

When Madison's turn came to dance, she did so elegantly and flawlessly to the music playing. Her attention was fixed on the dance and only the dance. She did the splits, countless twirls, and flips in her dance. She exited the stage after her dance and awaited the results in anticipation.

The judges announced the placings after a brief discussion. Madison had once again taken first place. She gave a firm nod without showing any sign of joy or excitement. She accepted her compensation in hand. She exhibited no emotion at all on her face. She simply approached her father.

"Let's go. I need to practice for the next competition," she said sternly as she began walking, expecting her father to follow her.

"But you just won a competition!" Nicholas exclaimed as he followed her.

"And?" Madison replied as she glanced at him.

"And you should take a break for once! I mean for the

past month you've done nothing but practice for competitions!" he replied with a hint of irritation in his tone.

"I'll take a break after the next one." She said as she walked. Nicholas sighed. "Promise?" He asked. Madison nodded. "Promise."

He had faith that Madison would be true to her word. She appeared to be mentally affected from all the practicing and dancing. It was really starting to worry him. A few days passed, and it was in the middle of the afternoon. Nicholas had planned on visiting Olivia today, he walked to Madison's room door. He knocked on the door.

"Hey Madison! I'm heading to the hospital to visit your mom! Are you coming?" he asked through the door.

"No, but I will next time!" she replied. Nicholas's eyes narrowed. He was too enraged to make an effort to persuade Madison otherwise. He believed she wouldn't even care if she knew how much Olivia wanted to see her. He sharply stormed out of the house and sped off to the hospital by himself. Madison was left to concentrate solely on her dance competition.

Nicholas parked his car and dashed inside the hospital to Olivia's hospital room. He sighed as soon as he entered. When Olivia heard him sigh, she looked around for Madison but couldn't find her. With a sad expression on her face, she stared at Nicholas.

"She didn't come this time either..?" she asked with a frown on her face.

Nicholas shook his head. "No. She's to fixated on her

stupid dance competitions. She rarely ever comes out of her room anymore, unless it's related to school!" He replied.

Olivia sighed before coughing a bit. "I was really hoping I would've gotten to see her." She said softly.

"After her next dance competition, she will. I'll make sure of it." Nicholas said firmly.

"I just miss her, Nicholas. I miss my happy, loving girl." Olivia said as a single tear dripped down her cheek. Nicholas frowned as he walked closer and wiped away Olivia's tear. "I do too." He replied as he held her hand in his.

Two more weeks went by, and it was the day of Madison's next dance competition. She was waiting for Nicholas downstairs with an irritated expression, ready to go. Despite Madison's diligence, he wasn't pleased with her at the moment as he made his way downstairs while glaring at her.

After a very tense car ride, they arrived at the studio, and Nicholas sat down while Madison went backstage. Nicholas found it annoying to have to repeat that cycle after it had already been done so many times. As Madison was stretching backstage, her eyes narrowed. She grumbled at the thought of her father, and the look he gave her. When the lights went down and the competition started, those thoughts quickly vanished from her head. Madison didn't even bother watching the other dancers, they were of no importance to her anyway.

When Madison's turn came to perform, she walked out onto the stage and took her place, only to discover that her father wasn't where he had been before. He wasn't even inside the auditorium. Madison danced despite feeling enraged because of Nicholas's absence. When her performance was over, she exited the stage and went to her father to fuss at him. When she left the auditorium, she discovered him standing outside the door.

"Why did you leave?! You didn't even see my performance!" Madison shouted sharply as she stormed over to her father. Slowly, Nicholas turned to face Madison. He was sobbing a lot and had tears streaming down his face.

"I left because the hospital called and told me your mother is dead!" He shouted back as tears continued to fall down his face.

Madison was taken aback by this. "Wait, what..?" She said softly with wide, watery eyes.

"She passed away an hour ago!" he yelled furiously as tears continued to fall. "All she wanted was to see you! Just once! But you were too fixated believing you could save her by winning stupid dance competitions that you never, not even once, thought about what she wanted!" He added, screaming at the top of his lungs at this point. He sighed, clenching his hands into tight fists as he looked at Madison, who looked horrified.

"I never should've let you continue dancing," he said firmly as he began to walk out of the building. In a panic, Madison followed him. Madison was filled with so many thoughts as tears streamed down her horrified face. She didn't realize it until now, but for a month and a half, she essentially neglected to visit her mother while she was in the hospital. While her mother was in pain, she didn't show her any love or attention at all. All Madison could feel right now was intense guilt.

After a few days had passed, Madison's mother was buried. The day had been the worst of her life. All Madison could think about as her mother lay there was the pain and suffering she had to endure. She also realized that the bond with her father would never be the same again.

Madison showed up at the dance studio for one last performance two weeks after the funeral, and nothing had ever been the same since. She entered the stage dressed entirely in white to symbolize lung cancer. One tear trickled down her cheek as she stood there in an elegant position. A small smile formed on her face when she saw snow falling out the window and gentle music begin to play.

BAD MEMORY

JOSH SHEA

Inspired by the painting "The Sick Room" by Edvard Munch

Andres was waiting in the park to meet up with his friend, Nina. She was always nice to him, even if he was rude. Nina has a big heart and loves taking care of others. Standing around five six, she was tall compared to others of her time. The pretty, dark hair she inherited from her mother detailed her facial features. They met up in the park very often. It was a beautiful landscape which they both enjoyed. An escape from the world as some would describe it.

"Andres, are you ready to go?"

"Of course," he said.

They lived in Kawah, Utah, just outside the central city. They planned to enjoy a quiet stroll. Andres knew this would be hard for Nina, given her adventurous personality. It didn't take long either. While walking, Andres was enjoying the peaceful evening but could tell Nina wasn't.

"I have an idea. Let's explore the Filmore Institute."

The Filmore Institute was an abandoned mental hospital, formerly for civil war veterans.

"That place terrifies me," he said.

After some persuading, Andres finally gave in. He hated the idea of going there but didn't want to say anything to Nina. They walked for a while and Andres made sure to enjoy nature while he could. Birds were singing such beautiful songs and the weather was perfect. Nina looked excited, Andres was happy when she was happy. The building looked very old and worn down. A smell of mildew filled the air outside the building.

"I always wanted to come here and see what it was like. My mom worked here a long time ago," said Nina.

"How come you never told me that?" asked Andres.

"I guess I never really thought about it," she said.

When entering the building, it seemed like it had been in use recently. It was massive. There were hundreds of rooms and tons of equipment everywhere. Andres was very intrigued by all of this. Nina looked happy to be here, which made Andres happy. They walked around together viewing all the rooms. Andres felt he and Nina were growing closer.

This is more joyous than he had been in years. When Andres walked past one, it stood out to him. He believed he saw a person in the room.

"Hello?" said Andres.

"Is someone in there?" he asked.

"Who are you?" asked the man.

"Get out of my room!" he yelled.

"What are you talking about?" asked Andre. Before his question could be answered, three men came sprinting down the hallway attempting to grab Andres. Before they could, he took off sprinting down the hallway. It was now filled with nurses and patients of all sorts. He had not seen them there before and continued to sprint past them. The men were in pursuit for a while until Andres found a room to hide in.

"What's going on?" he said to himself.

Andres hid for quite some time. He heard people going past the door and conversations about a psycho-patient in the institute. This puzzled him, due to the fact he was still under the impression it was abandoned. Those men chasing him seemed to be some sort of security. During this time, Andres realized Nina was gone. When he fled he didn't notice her following him. This worried him and encouraged him to exit his hiding spot. Upon leaving the room, the hallways seemed empty again.

Andres yelled out for Nina with no response. He continued to do so until he believed he found him. But instead of Nina a tall man appeared from a corner claiming I needed to go with him.

"Where's Nina?" asked Andres.

"Nina?" said the man.

"Where is she?" he repeated.

"You need to come with me," the man claimed.

Out of fear, Andre leaped at the man knocking him to the floor. He continued yelling at him demanding to know Nina's whereabouts. More men began to fill the hallways running after Andres. He fled the scene sprinting down the hallways until he believed he lost them. Finally coming to a stop, he smacked into someone coming around a corner.

"Nina?" he said

"Where did you go?" he asked.

"Why would you run Andres, you caused that man problems and the staff," she said.

"What do you mean?" he asked

"It's time for you to go back to your room."

The hallways were filled once more and everyone's attention was on Andre. Familiar sounds of footsteps followed, leading to the men capturing Andre. He felt a sense of betrayal from Nina. The trust built was gone from what he believed. Exhausted from everything that had happened, Andres blacked out.

Upon waking up, Andres smelled a soft lavender scent in the air. The air was warm and relaxing wherever he was. He had dreamed of him and Nina enjoying an evening together in the park. When he opened his eyes, there was a crowd of people standing around him.

"I can't believe his memory is getting so bad," said one man.

"The pain of memory loss must be unbearable," said another.

Andres wondered if they spoke about him. He remembered everything so clearly that he found it hard to believe they could be referencing him.

"Who are you people?" Andre asked.

"We're your family," said one little boy.

"But I don't have a family," he claimed.

"It's hard to believe that you don't remember your own children," said a woman. She reminded him of Nina.

"Where's Nina?" asked Andre.

"The nurse Nina?" asked another from the crowd.

Before they could answer the questions, two women entered the room. Nina was standing just across the bed from Andres. He wanted to speak to her but couldn't find the words.

"Are you ready for your medicine Andres?" Nina inquired.

Not being able to fathom reality, he just closed his eyes. All along not knowing she was just a nurse, he felt a sense of betrayal.

"Are you real?" asked Andres.

She waited to respond, with a sad expression on her face.

"Yes, I am."

"I think you need some rest, Andres."

Andres didn't speak again, for he had no reason to. He began thinking back on the times with his wife. Being reminded of the fact she was dead was the only thing he could piece together thoroughly. His family continued trying to talk to him but he didn't care. Their words meant nothing realizing Nina was gone. He thought of how easy it could be to go see her through death. Andres was willing to go to that point. Upon hearing the kind things his family was talking about, he frowned upon himself for thinking such thoughts. Even if he couldn't remember them very well, he felt he should be there for him. Especially since they are willing to come visit him. Hours after they left, Andres was escorted outside to the park and allowed to enjoy nature. Hearing the wind blow and leaves rustling, helped him to remember times from long ago. The family visited him earlier, he remembered all of them and the times they enjoyed together. Pondering upon the ideas of love, he remembered his wife whom he loved dearly. At this time Nina was hardly a thought to him. Life was a thrill and an enjoyment while he lasted. No more time to remember, he just wanted to enjoy the moments.

"I am ready to go back now," said Andre.

"Me, too," replied Nina.

Andres went to sleep that night looking forward to new memories but never woke up in the morning.

WE BECAME BLIND

PEYTON SMITH

Inspired by the painting "The Lovers" by Rene Margritte

PROLOGUE:

The bustling New York streets filled with busy bodies; all people holding different purposes. Some are simply trying to get to work, some are simply strolling the streets. But not Tatum. She had one task. Find one of the infamous Italian mobsters, Richard Kingston. He was the head of what was supposed to be a top-secret mission by the name of "CHILD." It was basically a human trafficking operation, and her job was to end it as soon as possible.

Tatum Monet's mother had organized a team of sorts. Its mission? To stop human trafficking and any bad deeds done to children. Because of this, Tatum was trained to be the best fighter, spy and asset her organization had ever seen. Her mother's whole cause of the operation was an ode to her late brother, Stanley. The pair were in fact trafficked children, but when her mother escaped, she never saw her brother again. So, with a striving hunger for revenge, she formed the organization "CHILD."

She read on her brown paper file that Richard should be just ahead, sipping the usual fruity drink like a child at the head of something so utterly terrible. When you get into this field, you realize horrible people are hiding in plain sight pretending to be everyone else. Tatum's motto is that you cannot trust anybody, sometimes not even your own blood. Some in her own workforce think she's heartless, but they won't be thinking such when they're dead and painted in betrayal.

Gripping the golden but rusted handle, she swung the door open, and entered the ever so casual bar. Goosebumps covered her pale arms from the outside chill, but also at the sight in front of her. The joint was unusually empty and darkened, and broken glass bottles littered the wooden floor. Her hand reached for her waistband immediately, and her eyes swiftly scanned the room. Something was not right about this. This bar usually has lines wrapped around the block with the building about to overflow with people. This had to be a ploy.

The air suddenly grew hotter as did her anxiety. Her hands shook slightly as she waved her tranq gun across the room. The sound of glass crunching under her Nike sneakers startled her, making her jump slightly. She breathed heavily, turning around different corners with fire in her veins. The worst type of missions were the mind games.

Her ears perked when she suddenly heard the sound of wind gushing and a powder type substance flooded the air, wafting right into her face. She instantly coughed and threw her head down, covering her face with her hands in hopes she could escape the tranquilizing drugs. Unfortunately, she knew she had failed when her balance started fading just like her vision. Her back hit the floor with a hard thud and she peered up to see a group of masked men sickeningly smiling down at her, holding her weapons.

DAY ONE

Luxurious jail cell, musty, and air as cold as ice was what she could describe the room as. Tatum had awoken from her unconscious state about an hour ago, and now she waited for any sign of life to reveal itself. The faint but irritating drip of the leaky faucet was getting to her head. This was the worst type of mental torture. She wanted answers. She had studied Richard's profile. She was sure he was not the head of this kidnapping operation, because the file simply stated it was not his style. However, she knew that once she found who had done this, their efforts would be humiliated by her spy-like expertise. Her mother would be furious with her for failing this miserably. You don't even want to know what happened to the last agent, must less her own daughter; her mother was cold hearted.

DAY TWO

"Get up," a stern voice ordered from above her sleeping form. Her eyes remained shut. An audible groan emitted from the man's throat. He mumbled something inaudible under his breath, but Tatum knew it was words of distaste. "I know you're awake, so either you give up this pitiful little charade, or I force you on your feet." Tatum's eyes still did not open. She wouldn't be told what to do. "Have it your way, then." He stated boredly. She could hear him heave a sigh before two rough hands met her pale arms and dragged her from her cot. She forced her body to go limp as he kept tugging on her body. He let out many groans as Tatum's eyes snapped open. As he slowly managed to lift her back to his chest, her leg swung behind her, successfully knocking the man back onto the ground. His arms slipped from her body, and she took the opportunity to run towards the open door. Just as her hand reached out at the doorknob, an angry hand laced around her ankle and tugged her down to the floor. She groaned in agony at the pain swelling in her knee and at her failed attempt to escape. His hands trapped her body to the ground as they both heaved in exhaustion. "I was gonna give you food, but you don't deserve it." His hand snaked around his back pocket and Tatum started to squirm at the sight of a syringe. She gave him a glare as he pierced the needle into her neck, and she was put into a deep sleep.

DAY FOUR

The metal table cooled her hands as they were chained together upon the desk. Her eyes bore into her guard's side profile. She discovered his name was Grayson because of the way his presumed Boss yelled his name. His eyes flicked over to her, sensing the way her eyes were glued to his face. He was met with a vicious glare that was the epitome of "if looks could kill." But fortunately, he liked to believe he was immortal. "Like what you see?" His voice was laced with sarcastic venom. Her eyes left his face and met the back of her head. She scoffed and laid back in the uncomfortable steel chair. She wanted to fire back a response but bit her tongue. She had already failed her mission, now her task was to collect as much information as possible from these strangers and escape. He let out an amused huff and looked at his Rolex watch for the time. When he glanced at it, an annoyed look took over the once amused expression. Tatum's eyebrows rose in curiosity.

Her curiosity was met with the door swinging open, and a rich old white guy approached her with a folder and ring adorned knuckles. A grunt left his lips as he sunk down into the chair next to her and glanced at his employee with appreciation. "Do you want to tell me who you are and why you got in the way of my operation?" She held her face blank and stared ahead of him. The Boss glanced at Grayson, indicating something Tatum could not decipher from her peripheral vision. He rose from his chair and stood behind her, his rough hands finding its way to both sides of her head, holding it harshly. She tried not to wince at the pressure. The man rolled up his sleeves and stood to face her as he adjusted the rings on his knuckles. "I'll make you talk."

DAY SIX

Even as she was sleeping she could feel the pulsating pain of the bruises that painted her face purple. It hurt to eat, talk and open her left eye. The day before, Grayson had made fun of her for the bruises in a cruel manner. They had gotten into small banter that day, but Tatum blew it off because of how hurt and exhausted she was. Her eyes kept closed as the door to her confinement opened slowly. Whoever this person was, they wanted to keep her peace or kill her silently. She was thinking the latter. The leather - clad boots thudded closer to her slowly and her body fell limp, ready to strike the second this unknown being approached her. *It was probably Grayson.* She thought bitterly. The shuffling of feet finally reached her bedside. Her hand slowly slid to the loosened bar she had taken off the cot. Gripping it tightly, she felt the presence lean right next to her bruised face. A whiff of cold air reached her face and she tensed when the feeling of an ice pack was placed on her cheek and eyelid. For once in her lifetime when around enemies, her guard let down. Just as she was processing what was happening, a rough hand laid itself on her head and let it glide through her brown locks. She opened her eyes just in time to watch her guard leave.

DAY EIGHT

Not much happened the day prior to Day Eight. The tension between Grayson and Tatum could be cut with a knife. They actually did not banter at all, which surprised Tatum the most. She was mostly surprised with how she couldn't come up with anything or even hate him. She hated herself for letting her guard down. She hated herself for getting taken. She hated herself for allowing this guy to get in her head, and slowly make his way into her heart. He had actually asked her about her normal life, outside of all the missions. *That was pretty stupid,* She thought. He himself was letting his guard down around her now too. He also gave her extra food yesterday. Today, she found herself sitting back in a small room, but this one sported rich paintings and velvet carpet. Too bad they'll have to scrub her blood out of it. Her face was still purple with the remnants of the beating she took a few days ago. It wasn't as bad as it could be, though, thanks to her not - so - scary guard. He stood behind her, standing silently with his hands behind his back as he waited for his Boss. His cologne hadn't stopped invading her senses ever since they entered the room. God, she couldn't get him out of her head and it drove her insane. She let out a sigh as she decided to address the elephant in the room. "I know you put the icepack on my face," she stated, confrontation present in her voice. At her words, she could hear him shuffle slightly, and start walking towards the vacant chair adjacent to her. She bit her tongue in nervousness, and clenched her fists together. He sat down next to her with a sign and looked into her eyes with an expression she could not decipher. If she had to take a guess, it could be hate or admiration. Maybe both. "Listen, Tatum. I hate you. I absolutely despise you." Her eyes widened slightly, and she tried to ignore the faint stabbing sensation in her heart. How could she be so stupid and gullible to actually feel something for the person who took her and kept her from her mission? The only good thing to come from all of this is the fact that she didn't tell him how she feels. Or felt, now. As much as she attempted to force it away, a saddened expression plastered itself onto her face. God, she hated this guy. His hazel eyes scanned her face swiftly, consuming the faint broken look she displayed. He sighed once more, before clearing his throat.

"Even though I hate you with every fiber in my being. You feel important to me. I don't feel how I'm supposed to feel around you. I've only known you for eight days but I can't get you out of my head. The way you take every beating like it's nothing, the way you just won't shut up when you're threatened with violence, and especially your passion for your job." Her once saddened expression flipped to shocked and happy? She didn't want to believe she could be feeling any sort of relief or joy from this, but she did. She was so surprised he had decided to pour his heart out to her this way. Her mouth opened to speak, and her voice cracked slightly as she did so. "I can't-"

She was cut off by the door swinging open and hitting the wall behind it harshly. The Boss strolled in, fury present on his face. Grayson sprung up from his spot beside her, his expression immediately darkening like he couldn't feel any of the emotions he just poured out. The Boss barely sent a glance his way as he made his way to Tatum, slamming his hands down before her. As soon as she slightly flinched at the motion, she was scolding herself for it. The Boss' disgusting breath reeked of alcohol as it blew in her shaken face. His yellow fingernails dug into the delicate pale skin of Tatum's forearms. She gritted her teeth in pain and disgust as she glared into his eyes. "Your 'team' has destroyed my entire Casino!"

His voice roared as his hand hit her cheek harshly. She let out a barely audible whine. His seething anger forced a wicked smile on his face and he bent down to whisper in her ear. His hand gripped her hair in a fistful and forced it backward to emphasize his point.

"But they didn't want you." He paused to laugh slightly before continuing.

"No, no. They found the man you were originally searching for, don't you worry. But when offering a trade deal for you, the head of your mission declined. How sad is that? But even sadder that it was your own mother." He tsked tauntingly. Tatum's eyes filled with tears at his harsh words. She knew her mother would do this to her. She just couldn't help but feel betrayed. The Boss let out another twisted laugh and patted her shoulder as he stood tall.

"You work for me now." She immediately shook her head in retaliation; jaw clenched and eyes furious with hurt and betrayal. He smiled, showing off his yellow teeth. He turned to walk out the door, speaking to her merrily as he exited the room. "I'm afraid you don't have a choice."

As the door slammed shut, the sob she tried to keep at bay broke loose from the dam that kept it in place. She wept silently as her cuffed hands met her eyes. She was so ashamed of how she was acting. She wasn't trained to be affected by her feelings. But she let her guard down and now the emotions were flooding her guarded walls. Fingertips met her slumped back and massaged gently, comforting the tears that rolled down her pink cheeks.

"It'll get better," he muttered, making it sound like it pained him to say, (which it probably did.) She choked out another sob at his words. He winced, clearly he had made it worse. He was fighting with himself over what to do besides simply escorting her back to her room. Maybe she would feel better if she knew his story. *No, that will probably have a worse reaction than the ones his words just produced.* He thought, "I want to go home." She sobbed in agony. His hands just kept comforting her solemn figure, closing his eyes and wincing at the sounds she was producing. Comforting people was definitely not his specialty. His eyes remained squeezed shut, but popped open once he heard her sobs subside and her soft hand lay itself over top of his.

DAY ELEVEN

The past few days have meshed together in a blur. Tatum and Grayson actually were starting to get really close and dive into their feelings for each other more. As fast as this "relationship" was moving, they felt as if they had known each other forever. When she was forced to train everyday, he would bring her extra food and give her more time to sleep. He would always step in if any of his co-workers or her trainer would cause any bit of harm her way. At his actions, many people started to get suspicious. Little did they know, word of this eventually reached the Boss.

"You're from Italy?" She gasped in amazement. She always wanted to visit Italy, and here was this guy who she was starting to adore, saying it's his home country. He nodded shyly at her question, tracing the lines of her palm in anxiety. An excited giggle left her mouth, making a smirk take over Grayson's face. "Maybe one day I'll take you there. When we can be free from this place."

He spoke sadly, making Tatum's mood die down slightly. A frown was now in place of her once excited smile. "How did you get roped into all of this anyway?" she asked nervously. This was it. This was the question he so desperately did not want her to ask.

"Well...." He trailed off, trying to find the right words to explain his story. Her hands folded over his comfortingly, giving a smile to urge him on. At that, he gained the courage to share.

"Back in Italy, I had no family. I was abandoned at a young age; no home, no food, no water. As I grew older, I had to do things to survive. Bad things. I had to-"

He cut himself off, sighing deeply and closing his eyes in remembrance of a seemingly disturbing event. Tatum's demeanor remained comforting, but she was intrigued to know more.

"I don't want to talk about it. But the Boss sought me out after hearing of those terrible things and took me from my spot in the alley. I woke up dazed and confused. All that he said to me when we first met was that I worked for him. I didn't have any say. I tried to escape but he would just hurt me to force me to stay. I don't want to see that happen to you, Tate."

His eyes flickered with sadness and anger. It felt weird to see him this way. This last week she discovered a noticeable change in his presence with her versus everyone else. She felt special, in a way. She felt special because she got to see his most vulnerable state, and he trusted her enough to shed it to her. Tatum let out a shaky breath at his story. He was just like her. He had never been entirely the bad guy. He was just doing what he was forced to. She had now become just like him. He sighed sadly, wrapping his strong arms around her weak figure, shoving her head into his chest.

"So sweet." An evil voice cooed from behind them. Their bodies separated from each other and their heads whipped around to face the Boss, cigar in hand and rings flickering in the harsh lighting. He turned behind him in the doorway and waved his fingers at his other employees. At the flick of his hand, the workers rushed in, hands gripping Tatum's arms tightly as they drug her out of the room kicking and screaming in protest. Grayson sprung from his spot on the bed, fingers reaching out for his newfound lover's outstretched hand, but she was pulled away from his reach. Some of his other co-workers took hold of him, dragging him behind Tatum. He didn't put up a fight; he wanted to be wherever she was.

He noticed the same room the Boss had once beat Tatum

in for hours while he stood there and watched. His face contorted into a dark expression at the sight. She was already in the room, he could hear her screaming and fighting as she was strapped into one of the chairs. His jaw clenched tightly as he was then brought into the room. His head immediately snapped to her direction, trying to find solace in her candy apple green eyes. But instead of her face he was met with a cloth woven bag placed over her head. She was hyperventilating, he could tell. One, because her chest heaved up and down. Two, because he knew she didn't like her face being suffocated. She explained to him one night that she was terrified of the blanket suffocating her, which at the time, he thought it was cute, but now her fear has become all too real.

He yelled out her name hoarsely, promising her that it would be alright as he was tossed into his chair roughly. They then yanked the bag on his head roughly, not a care in the world that this was once their co-worker. A chilling mood entered the atmosphere of the room when he could hear Tatum's painful screams. He could hear the smack of rings against skin. It infuriated him. It kept continuing, until finally they ceased and the Boss' heavy breathing was the most prominent sound to be heard. His fancy shoes scuffed their way over in front of him, and Grayson could sense him lean down to his covered face.

"All of *this is* a weakness. A disgrace. You are a stain to my name and legacy." Just as the swing of a punch almost landed on his face, one of his co-workers interfered nervously.

"Sir, we're under attack, we need all forces up to the Casino." An angered sigh left the Boss' mouth as he rushed out of the room, co-workers trailing behind him. He simply stated that his job was not done as he rushed out of the room. Now, the couple? Was left alone and all that was on Grayson's mind was *her*. She breathed heavily and cried at the same time. He knew Boss must've hurt her really good. What he wouldn't give to end him. He scooted his chair over to her side since he didn't have anything to free himself of the cuffs with. Her breathing increased as the pain still pulsated. She had to calm down or she would suffocate.

"Hey, hey, hey. It's alright, just breathe. Talk to me, do anything." He pleaded. She tried to talk but her words meshed together and her sobs mixed with her breathing. Things were getting worse. In a second, an idea popped into his head. He was hoping that her lips were where he was headed.

His hidden face swooped down to her clothed lips and attached through the thin material of the bags. Everything in her brain stopped. She suddenly forgot that she was previously hyperventilating under this dirty cloth, and her eyes fluttered close, relaxing into the heartwarming kiss. She broke apart first, breathing slowly. He pulled away, hands slightly shaking nervously.

"I, uh, read that to stop panic attacks, kissing can work because you're not focused on just breathing. I-I'm sorry if I overstepped anything or-"

"Stop talking, Grayson." He was cut off by her lips

meeting him once more. He smiled delicately into the kiss. This was definitely not what they expected when they first met each other, but fate works in mysterious ways. Their second kiss was short lived as the door creaked open and their heads whipped to the source of the sound. Grayson was ready to give up his life if they hurt her again. Tatum's eyes adjusted to the bright light once the bag was lifted from her head. She glanced up to see one of her mother's workers. Even more joy found its way to her expression, making her laugh in relief. Grayson's form slumped as he let his guard down at her joyful laugh. She was set free from her confinement, and soon Grayson was as well. He enveloped her in a large hug, finally kissing without their faces hidden.

EPILOGUE:

Tatum' wine glass swished around in her glass cup, a bright smile peering back at her lover, Grayson. The boat ride he has taken her on was what made her love him and Italy even more. She's just glad that he held onto his promise. It's been almost a year since she was first taken by his group, but they grew stronger with each passing day. Their love had never faded. He asked her to marry him a month ago. That's why they were in Italy, planning their venue. Her mother allowed her to leave her association. Despite Tatum's hateful thoughts about what would happen to herself, her mother was very understanding and did not rip her a new one for her failed mission. As they kissed under the twinkling starlight of Italy, their love burned as bright as the stars, just as it always had. They just had to search for it.

FOREST

AIYANA SUTHERLAND

Have you ever had an environment or place that you could never get tired of, no matter the amount of times you visit? That's exactly what a small, trench-like forest behind my old home was for me. The forest behind my previous home in Campbellsburg had always been a safe space for me ever since I could remember, it provided a peaceful and calming environment to stay in and had been a small place of beautiful scenery that never got boring to see and experience.

This forest changed and shifted just as I did over the years. In the Summer and late Spring months, its tall trees and flower bushes were lush, green, and full of life. The birds sang its song of beauty, and the snakes, cats, and mice claimed it as home just as I did. In the Fall and Winter months, the forest was full of vibrant, red-scale colors. The animals hurry through the forest floor in preparation for the upcoming season of Winter, birds leaving their nests nearing the beginning of the colder months, and soaring the skies in search of warmer temperatures. During the winter, the birds no longer sang their songs, the life leaving the forest and leaving behind a peaceful, calm, serene, and temporary graveyard. When the forest was left barren, snow coating the forest floor, the forest revealed its hidden and long-lost items. Every year, there was always something new to find deep within the confines of snowy branches of the forest, becoming a common look for the wooded area. Whenever you were within the confines of the forest, you felt a sense of belonging, safety, and peace. If you provided the forest with respect and care, you would be given that same respect in return. The forest would care for you just as it cared for all the other woodland creatures it accepted with open arms, and provide you a place to escape and feel safe and protected. Its gentle winds would comfort you, and its birds' songs would soothe your mind of any stress. The forest's kindness knows no bounds, and you never have to be fearful of whatever nature provides.

"A walk in nature, walks the soul back home" - Mary Davis. I have many fond memories of the forest, one of my favorite ones being one day when I was about 10, I and two of my closest friends snuck back there during the winter months without my parents knowing, even if we were forbidden from entering the forest after our parents found out glass panes and other dangerous debris was thrown down in it. We were scavenging for the parts to an old tree house that we threw out to use the ladder for a staircase onto the trampoline when I was about 6 years old, and instead, we happened to stumble upon a family of cats, all of which seemed to be wild street cats. They were all living by an older house which was near the western border of the wooded area, and we noticed that other people who may live there were leaving out food for them. This began a common tradition of sneaking into the forest late into the day, just before the streetlight curfew, and offering up whatever food that we had on us that day to the mother cat and her baby kittens. Eventually, those cats began to see us as their family in a sense, welcoming us into their home and letting us feed and pet them without fear. It was a nice memory I will always keep in my mind, which reminded me that the forest isn't just a pretty place to run rampant, it is home to both scary and unpredictable, adorable creatures. That was when I first truly realized that I could make this forest an extension of my home. A place to love, and appreciate.

"Nature is not a place to visit. It is home." - Gary Shyder. Another pleasant memory of the forest would be when we made our "fort". This turned out to be a place right on the edge of the tree line, where old branches had fallen and formed a small enclosed area, and I and my friends thought it was perfect to build off of. I knew that we couldn't just take blankets out of the house and throw them into the forest and plan to keep them there, so we had to make do with what we had. We searched around and eventually found the pile of old Christmas evergreen trees, along with the bonus of old debris from various sources. With this, we got to work. We decided that we would use old playground debris to support the wood we would end up using as walls and the roof, and the Christmas tree branches for supporting, and creating new, walls. I remember being proud of that small fort that we made, seeing the messy craftsmanship and small interior, and thinking that it was practically a work of art. To me, it was like a small castle, one that we made all by ourselves. We would often visit that fort that we built, adding to it more and more each time. It was a project that never got boring, and it felt as if we were able to build our own home within the forest, along with the other animals and vegetation.

"In your arms, I find Solace and comfort, my safe place." - Unknown. Although the forest was a thing of beauty and fun, not every memory of the forest can be a happy one. This one is from the first winter I visited the forest frequently. It was cold, snowy, and the ground was blanketed in a thin sheet of frost and powdery snow. All was quiet. At least, everything but the house I had fled from moments before. I had a loose coat thrown on and had managed to snag my boots and run out the door as a parental figure fought with my sisters. As I entered the usual trench that me and my friends would often explore through, I sat by the big tree that rested in its center. I was met with a soothing silence, one that I had been searching for all night long. I never realized before that moment, feeling the snow fall onto my face, that the forest could feel so safe and calm as it did that night. I spent at least an hour out in the cold winter weather, not minding the temperature, just enjoying the scenery. After this incident, my trips down to the backyard forest became more common, and when a family fight happened, that's where I'd be. The place provided a strange sense of comfort that I was unable to get at home, and it will always be my safe space, of which I feel like I can run to, and shield myself from my troubles.

"Time spent amongst the trees is never wasted time." - Katrina Mayer. As of today, the forest in my old backyard will always be a safe place within my heart, even if I don't have that much time to stop by and visit any longer. Even so, I will always plan to visit that forest every chance I get, either to remind myself of the good times I had during my childhood, or to simply feel a change of pace. Whatever the reason may be, I will never forget what that place means to me, and how it has helped me both as I grew up, and even now. I hope to take a walk through the old forest again this year when I go see some of my family back in Campbellsburg for Christmas, even if it might not be the same as I remember. I hope to be able to find that same sense of peace I once did in that serene forest as I once did all those years ago. Even if I don't, it'll be nice to visit old memories.

THROUGH MY EYES

SARA TREECE

Inspired by "The Sphere" by M.C Esher

5 **years ago…**

I can't wait to be out of this school forever. Only a few more hours until they call my name to cross the stage. "Congratulations Christian Atwell" and then I'm out of this place. Everyone here just treats their lives like they have more than one. Putting all of themselves out there into the world. Only worrying about popularity and relationships. There is so much more to life than that. Ridgewood Private is an awful place. *You just wish someone like you could find a person who understands us.* Shut up, Shadow. Nobody would understand. No one ever understands. I have only ever found one person to understand, and he'll be out of my life after college starts.

Nico Perez is pretty cool. He keeps to himself. I appreciate people like Nico. You know, the ones that aren't petty and in all sorts of drama. Those types of people are scarce these days. Nico and I have been friends for quite some time. We try to avoid as much drama as we can. I have it a little easier than Nico though. Having Elena Perez as a sister would make it a million times harder to not be brought into drama.

"Nico, what did you do with my headphones?! You know I need those for school. I'll be caught dead before I use those embarrassing school earbuds!" Elena went on about her stupid headphones for another 30 minutes before realizing she had left them on the bathroom counter.

Nico and Elena always fight with each other about things. Especially if it's about Gabriel Padettis.

Elena and Gabriel have hung out once or twice but Gabriel is an abusive and awful person. Elena got out of the situation but sometimes he still won't leave her alone and Nico steps in. Nico and I have never liked Gabriel, and what he did to Elena made him unbearable. The reason I know so much is because Nico and I hang out a lot. I think we are very similar and can relate to each other. *Just wait until he finds out about us.* He's not going to, he would not understand. The only people that know are me and you.

Everyone else in my life thinks I have this thing called schizophrenia, but I know that's not true. I have done my research and I don't hallucinate things. I don't have the right symptoms to be diagnosed with schizophrenia. Throughout the years of research, I have only ever found one thing that makes sense. It's called dissociative identity disorder. It's a very rare disorder that is almost always misdiagnosed. But I know this has to be what it is. Nico doesn't really understand it, but he believes me. He is the only one to ever believe in me. The only person to not just look at me and see a mentally ill person. I don't know how my life is going to be without him.

I guess we'll find out.

Present Day...

"το κακό ξύπνησε"

I wake up and see Phantom. "Long time no see" he says to me. "It's good to be back." I say to him, hoping he will give me my assignment. I need to feel the cold night's breeze on my face while I go to find the next person. *No, don't do it please. You know it isn't right, please just stop. Let me out, Shadow! Please let me out!* Shut up Christian, you already know how this goes. Nothing you say will change anything. I feel the need to kill. I enjoy it. Get over it.

"Tonight, Hugo Perez is your victim," Phantom says to me. Harvey (Phantom) Bridger is one of my favorite people in the world. He lets me do what I am destined to do. *No this is wrong Shadow, you know you shouldn't do this. You know it's wrong.* Christian, your bickering is not going to change reality, so make our life easier and shut up.

"We are going to war with the Spanish, Shadow, they are becoming too much of an inconvenience for my business.

This murder tonight will start a war that you can finish." The corners of my mouth rose as he was saying these words. I finally feel like myself again.

"I'm aware you already know the location," he tells me. I know exactly where to go. I spent all of my days inside that house, trapped inside Christian's dimwit head. "Yes sir, I know exactly where to go." Another smile comes across my face because I get to do what I have been dreaming of for years. *Please don't do it, Shadow. Don't kill Mr.Hugo. He was always so acceptive of us, don't do it. I'm begging you.* Please, you think I care about his acceptance? Ha, I have wanted to kill him since the first time you forced me to listen to hours of his nonsense.

I start my way out of headquarters and walk about 4 blocks to the Perez house. The only good thing about being trapped in Christian's head for so long was that I knew the house, and where everyone is in it. I also remember that the Gambler always sits out on the back porch every night. *Don't call him that. His name is Hugo Perez, not the Gambler. Shadow just because he's competition with your boss doesn't mean you have to do this.* Have to? Please. I want to do this, Christian. Now stop talking, you know I hear nothing when I kill, so it does you no good.

I arrive at the house. It's about midnight, the best time of night. The city is sleeping, but I feel the most alive. I can smell the cigar coming from the back. I know exactly what I am going to do. I start to walk by the side of the house, making my way to the back. Gambler is on a phone call. Even better. I hold back a laugh because he is just making this too easy on me. I mean come on, this wouldn't even be enjoyable if it wasn't for the person I get to kill. Eh, beggars can't be choosers.

He's on the edge of the porch, his chair facing away from me. So I start to, you know, kill him. I had his neck grasped in one hand, my other hand free.

"Having fun yet?" He says to me as he gasps for air.

"Evil is like a shadow." I smile and say back to him.

Job complete. For now. I'm sure my week will be pretty busy whenever Enzo, Nico, and Elena find their father. Can't wait.

The next morning...

I hate this. I hate it so much. I want him to be gone, please just get out of my head. I'm not that person. I'm not the one who killed my best friend's father. I need him gone. *How do you think I feel? Always nagging. It'd be nice to just be me. I wonder if there's a way to do that? Maybe Phantom would know since he knows how to bring me out of your stupid head.* I don't want to do this anymore. I need it to stop. I can't watch you kill all of these innocent people. *Innocent? Gambler was hardly innocent. His family, just the same as him. Especially that daughter of his. Who would've thought that the princess of Ridgewood Private would become one of the best assassins the world has ever seen?*

Stop talking about Elena. Stop talking at all. *Elena? No, her name is Blade now haven't you heard? I'm guessing you could infer why she goes by blade.* Just stop it. Her name is Elena, it will always be Elena. *Yeah, keep telling yourself that. You hear she killed that abusive guy's dad? Gabriel Padetti was it? 23 stabs was the final count. Guess she got her revenge there.* I am done talking about this. Just leave me alone. I've had enough of all the murders; I just want to sleep.

I try to sleep but barely can. Every time I close my eyes I can see theirs. All of his victims right before he takes their life. Just on replay in my mind. Every second, every minute, every hour, every day. I try to avoid sleeping because I never know if I am going to wake up as me or as him. I can't help it, I am so tired.

That night...

"I have some news for you, Shadow. The Perez's found Gambler this morning and are on their way to uncovering who did it. Be ready for one of the sons to come your way." My body fills with excitement as I know soon enough that Nico will find out I did it. I know he won't be able to kill me. He loves me. Or at least this idiotic excuse for a human. *He won't believe I did it. He is the only one who sort of understands this entire situation. He will know it was you and not me. He will know that I would never do that. And he will know that I would want him to end it rather than have all of these people die.*

Oh, enough of this pity party. Nobody cares but you, Christian. You better just hope nobody comes after you instead of me because I think you and I both know how that would end up. And I do not want to die. *If Nico comes to me and tries to kill me I will let him. The world would be a better place without you.*

Next thing I know, Enzo is yelling my name. Or really he is yelling "Christian I will kill you!" Ha, so dramatic. He never grew out of that one. Nico is pathetic. Sending his own brother to do his dirty work. Pathetic. And a death sentence. I mean, let's be real. Enzo Perez, is not an assassin. He is just a puny young adult, full of anger because his daddy died. That one was always weak. *Shut up, Shadow, you murdered his father. I would kill you if I could.*

"Hey buddy" I say to Enzo.

"I will kill you. My father didn't deserve that!" He glares at me. What he doesn't know is that his father did deserve it.

"You know your precious daddy was a money launderer, correct?" I scoff.

"You think I live in another world? Of course I knew that. I know everything about my family."

"Oh, so you also know that you will not come out of this alive?" I say to him.

"I gotta at least try Christian," he whimpers to me.

"I'm not Christian. God, I hate when people call me Christian."

"Wait, what do you mean?" he looks at me with confusion. I guess he never knew about it. Oh well.

"Any last words?" I ask him.

"I won't die without a fight." He yells as I laugh.

"Evil is a shadow." I say, just as he gasps for his last breath, just like his Dad did. Oh, the irony.

Two down, how many more are stupid enough to cross me? Guess we'll find out. *I will not let you kill Nico or Elena. I will do whatever it takes.* Please like you could stop me. Plus, Blade is not that bad. I fancy Blade. A hot assassin that isn't afraid to fight to the death. That's my kinda girl right there. *Shut up Shadow. You would only ever be bad for her. Plus you murdered her father and her brother. I don't think you'd have much of a shot.* We'll see about that.

Since my job is done for the night, I am going to go blow off some steam at Ferly's. Best bar in the city. Well, maybe not the best but definitely the cheapest and closest. Only about a 3 minute walk away from headquarters. That's what I love about New York, everything is so close together I usually don't need a car to get anywhere. I start walking to the bar when I hear sounds of struggle coming from what used to be a warehouse. It's abandoned now, which is why muffled screams are unusual.

When I step into the entrance, I follow the sound to its source. I was surprised, so to speak, when I see a very familiar face. The face of a very dashing, lovely assassin. The only thing irregular about this was that she was the one tied to the chair. I was confused for a second. Did whoever bring her here just leave her to die? I got my answer seconds later when I heard a familiar voice.

"I bet you regret murdering my father right about now don't you Elena?" Gabriel Padetti yells from somewhere in the warehouse. She looked up at me. But there wasn't fear in her eyes, only anger. I hold my hand up signaling to her to wait.

I get out of sight to see what this Gabriel is intending to do before he miserably fails. You think I am going to let this fiery piece of beauty die? Ha, not likely. *I'm not even going to say anything, at least you want to save her.* Finally, after about 10 seconds Gabriel returns to the scene with what looks like a blade. How unoriginal could this pathetic, no good, abusive excuse for a person, be? Very is the answer to that. You can't out do the (second) best assassin in the world by simply using the same weapon as her.

"Are you ready to die Elena? How does it feel to be on this side of the Blade?" says Gabriel. "Oh that's right, I forgot you can't speak!" he says while laughing.

"Okay this is just getting boring at this point." I say, walking out of the shadow I was standing in. Gabriel whips his head around when he hears my voice.

"Christian?" he says with a certain stutter in his voice.

"God, I hate when people call me that. Just like she probably hates when people call her Elena." I said to him,

"Wait what? So who are you?" he asks me.

"Don't worry about that." I say walking towards him. He starts to hold the blade up to me. I laugh at his pathetic face. "Come onnnnn Gabriel, you really think that puny thing will stop the world's best assassin? The answer is no." He suddenly just drops it and freezes in his place. I pick up the blade he drops and quickly swing my arm down to cut Blade free of the rope around her body. Gabriel flinched as I did this. I suppose he thought I was going to stab him instead.

"Aw Gabriel, you thought I was going to stab you? No. That's not my forte. It is hers though, as I'm sure you know." I say this while I give Blade the weapon.

"Hi Gabe." Blade says as she stands up and takes a few steps forwards. Gabriel starts to back away. "Oh not so fast honey. I owe you one. You did catch me by surprise, I'll give you that. But now, I'm afraid it's too late for you." she says. Wow I've never seen someone like that before. The way she moves is mesmerizing. Gabriel tried to run away. Let's just say he didn't escape her. She knows her way around a blade that's for sure. After she's finished with Gabriel she turns to me.

"So what about you, killing my brother and my father. What do you have to say for yourself?"

"It's just business, nothing personal."

"If I knew better, I would kill you right now. But I don't." she says to me. A smile appears upon my face. "Your smile's not bad but don't tempt me, Atwell." she starts to walk away from me.

"You're welcome" I say to her. She whips her head around quickly.

"What were you expecting? A thank you? Please." She rolls her eyes.

"I mean I did save your life." When I say this she laughs. Oh, what a beautiful smile.

"You didn't save my life," she snarks at me.

"Okay sure." I say with sarcasm. She looks back at me one last time and then walks out of the building. Now, I head to the bar.

The next day...

God I wanted to throw up when you were being hypnotized by that cold hearted killer in Elena's body. *Shut up, dimwit.* Oh, trust me I would've not listened if I could've. It's not like I had a choice. I can't believe she is who she is now. I mean at least when you kill people there isn't that much blood. She enjoyed that too much for my liking. Well, not that I like it at all, but still it was disturbing to see someone from my childhood doing something like that.

Quit being so judgmental, Christian. Especially of Blade. She is perfect. Oh, bite me Shadow. *You should just be glad Phantom hasn't made me permanent because I would pursue her as soon as your boneheaded voice wasn't in my mind.* Yeah and how would you manage to do that? *Oh so I guess you don't listen to everything Phantom says.* What do you mean? *I guess you'll have to wait and see.*

Midnight...

"Welcome, Shadow." Phantom says to me. Something feels different. He didn't say welcome back. He always says welcome back. I feel lighter, but empty. Something is missing. Do you feel that too? Christian? Hello? I look at Phantom with confusion written all over my face. He laughs and says something that sends a shock wave through my entire body.

"How does it feel being free of Atwell?" He eyes me.

"Wait, how did you do it? I thought you were joking when you said you could get rid of him." I say.

"I'm the boss, Shadow. I am the boss." he says while walking away from me. He leaves the room. Leaving me there, alone, and in complete silence.

Nothing is in my head. He is gone. Christian is finally gone! I can't believe it. I really can't believe it. After all the years, I am in control. I can do what I want. I can go for whoever I want. It just hit me. Blade. I have to find her. I need to find her.

I leave headquarters to search for her. First, I walk around the city just trying to find any sign of her. Any clues that could lead me to her. But I found nothing. Not one bit of something. I go to her family's house, nothing. That place was oddly quiet. Not one person was there. As I walk away it hits me. She's just like me. And I know exactly what I do when I am preparing to kill. I also know that I technically killed two of her family members. All of a sudden, I feel a cold sharp object on my neck.

"Hi, lovely" I say with a smile on my face.

"Don't call me that, Atwell." she says to me.

"I am not Atwell. I am Shadow."

"Ha. Shadow. What a pathetic name for someone who is nothing more than a weak little schizophrenic boy." she says to me.

"You never knew, did you?" I say to her in a concerned voice. She then removes her blade away from my neck.

"What are you saying?" she asks me.

"I am Shadow. Christian is gone, and he's not coming back. He was my other person, or I suppose I was his since he had more control over me. But not anymore." When I say this to her, a look of realization floods her face.

"So you're not Christian." she says.

"Correct. I am Shadow, the world's best assassin." Blade looks at me with confusion once again.

"You definitely are not the world's best assassin, much less New York's best assassin. I have that title and intend on keeping it." Her confidence is charming.

"I doubt that you will be able to do that." I say to her.

"Okay let's make a deal, whoever has the most clean kills in 3 days can be named the better assassin. If it's me, you have to be my personal assistant. You name your prize." She says to me. I know exactly what I want.

"You." I say locking my eyes with hers. I can tell she is flustered but she doesn't want to show it.

"Okay a deal is a deal. Meet back at the warehouse in 3 days." she says to me. She then turns around and walks away slowly. She knew what she was doing, but so did I.

Three days later...

I show up to the warehouse around 11:45. I'm never early to things but I was eager to see the results of tonight. 15 minutes go by and she still doesn't show. I begin to worry at this point because she could have been playing me the entire time. I've never felt this way before. Then again, I never really had the opportunity to until now.

Ten more minutes go by and my hope starts to fade into sadness. Only 5 more minutes, then I'm leaving. This is already pathetic enough. That's it, I'm leaving.

I start to walk out of the warehouse when I hear her voice.

"Hey, giving up so soon?" Blade had been there watching me the whole time. Watching me make a fool of myself, looking miserable because she didn't show up. God, I should've known better. Well, there is nothing I can do about it now.

"No, just tired of wasting my time." I say with uncertainty in my voice.

"So, what's your final count?" I asked her. "Zero" she tells me while starting to smile. In that moment I realized that she wanted me too. She didn't kill anyone. She wanted me to win the deal. I can't believe it.

"So, where to now?" she asks me while walking towards me.

"Back to my apartment." I say. Then I ask her, "I didn't ever think you would want to be with me."

"I never liked Christian, but you, you don't seem too bad Shadow." She says as she looks up at me. This is weird, I am never happy, but I feel happy right now. I don't know what to say.

"I also am fond of your extracurricular activities. We will have a lot of fun together."

A woman after my own heart.

MEMOIRS

A BOND WORTH MORE THAN ANY BANNER

BREANNA PERKINS

"Two hearts, each unique and imperfect, came together to create a bond that is stronger than the sum of its parts." - Unknown. Many people say you can't have a strong bond with animals but I don't see it this way. I have a bond that is like no other with a bull named Axel. Now there are tons of animals I could write about our bonds, but Axel has made the biggest impact in my life. This all started long before he was even born. He has so many nicknames but my favorites are Handsome, A Man, and Axe. He is so unique but his looks are the biggest part of his unique self.

Axel is a Hereford bull meaning he is mostly Red with a white face, brisket, and stomach. He has a huge head and pigment around his right eye. Kind of like a pirate with an eye patch. This bull has the biggest dopey eyes and almost always has his ear forward. Axel has a wonderful gold nose ring that fits him so perfectly. His tail is long and "steamy" like he hasn't washed his hair in a year but it has red and black streaks of hair going through his switch. Little white "socks" go up his legs like he's ready to go at any time.

Personality varies so much between cattle but A-Man has the biggest personality of all. Talking is his favorite thing to do. I love it cause we have whole conversations with each other. If I have a bad day I tell him all about it and he responds to me every time. Sometimes I feel like he truly knows what I am saying, it's kind of creepy. If you need Axel to do something, get some beet pulp. He will do anything for a nice handful of beet pulp and he will go crazy if you don't get it to him fast enough. When he was a show bull I got him a $2.50 ball from Walmart. That was the best money spent. He loves that ball and loves to play it with me. I'll roll it to him and he will roll it back for as long as I play with him. He is so social so putting him by himself is a terrible option. He will play with anything he can find which normally ends up getting him in trouble. Babysitting all the little calves is his favorite thing to do until he runs out of energy but the calves are still going. Our incredible bond started in November 2021.

I was so excited on October 30, 2021, as I had just bought his mom. I brought her home the next day and got to watch her baby move inside of her womb. Spice, his mother, wasn't due until January 2, 2022. As I was waiting for him to make his arrival I would always fist bump him on the side where he would sit in the womb. Half the time he would bump back and the other half he was asleep. I checked cows every day so fist-bumping him was a priority otherwise it wasn't a good day. I fell in love before I even met him.

My first true memory was on January 2, 2022, when I palped Spice, his mom, I got to feel him "fist bump" me with his hoof. That was the coolest thing ever. That night as I was lying in bed I came across the name Axel and fell in love with it and I immediately knew that's what the baby's name was going to be if Spice had a bull. It was a snowy day the next day so I got to sleep in. When I finally woke up I saw a text from my dad and the guy who owns the property where my cattle lived. It was a picture of Spice and a "fresh" little bull baby in the barn. I called him Axel before I even met him. When I got to the barn later that morning, I was so excited. Axel and Spice were sitting together in the corner so I went and sat down with them. He put his head on my lap and fell asleep, from that moment on I knew just how special he was going to be. Little did I know that a normal day was going to turn into one of the best days of my life.

State Fair is a show that can either go well or be the biggest joke ever. This year was the best year ever though. I remember sitting in the stall leaning up against him and he put his head on my chest. He fell asleep for forty-five minutes. so many fair goers loved it and I loved having that extremely special moment for us. The next day I had to "fit" him, make him look all nice and pretty with a lot of hair spray. I had never fit an animal completely by myself before.

When I was told I had to fit him by myself I freaked out. He had never had his legs clipped let alone fit before. I got down on my knees and started fitting away. He stood there like the king he is and I couldn't be more proud of him. "Class 48 Herefords the ring" It was our time to shine. A truck had caught fire outside and was put out with a fire truck. As Axel and I made our way outside a dumb person purposely spooked Axel. He jumped then slipped to land very hard on his knees losing all the hair out of it. He still doesn't have hair to this day. I panicked as his knees started to bleed, he was very light on his front legs now. I got him to the show ring and showed him to my dad. Thankfully, he rested for a bit in the makeup ring and started to walk comfortably again. He came out of the thing placing third place. It was such a chaotic day, but such a good day. I showed him for another year after that, making so many more wonderful memories. It was his last show and time for the next chapter.

As Axel retired from his show career I was broken but I get to spend time with him daily. He lives a wonderful life out in the pasture with as many cows as he could ever want. I even sneak him into the barn to blow him off and play with him. He is now almost two years old. I can not believe how fast the last two years have been but man have they been such good years. Just because it doesn't seem like a normal bond doesn't mean it won't be the most amazing bond you've ever had. I promise it's worth a try in the end to give them all a chance.

PAP'S BOY AND THAT'S IT

NOLAN PRATHER

> "What children need most are the essentials that grand-parents provide in abundance. They give unconditional love, kindness, patience, humor, and lessons in life" - Rudy Giuliani.

My grandfather Pete, "Pap," was my favorite person ever. His stories always fascinated me, and I have tried to model myself after him. Pap was a shorter man, around 5'10, at least before he started shrinking, with only a little curly white hair left on his head, and a long, white handlebar mustache that would make Hulk Hogan jealous. His low, scratchy voice was easily recognizable when he would enter the room asking, "What's going on 'round here?" You would instantly know that Pap had arrived. Everyone adored him; he told stories in ways only he could, never missing an opportunity to crack a joke and send the whole house into laughter. The part of Pap that will always stick with me is how compassionate and understanding he was with everyone he met, which leads me to one of my favorite memories with Pap.

"Dad was a great man... He loved everyone, especially his grandkids" - Brooks Prather.

Once when I was around 9-10, Pap took me to the store with him to pick up groceries. While we were there, he ran into someone he had served with in the Navy. When Pap asked him what he had done after boot camp, the veteran explained he had gone AWOL just months after being stationed in Florida. The veteran seemed younger than Pap, but I could've sworn they were related. He also rocked an awesome mustache, and spoke in a raspy voice; although, he talked much louder than Pap, almost yelling. It later occurred to me that, like many veterans, he probably had hearing problems. Pap and I spent 20-30 minutes chatting with the man, and I remember being fascinated as to why he went AWOL. When I asked him, he responded "I was homesick... 20 years old and I felt alone". On the way home, Pap seemed quieter than usual, like he was thinking hard about something. "What's wrong Pap?" I asked. "Y'know Nolan, it doesn't make sense that he is not considered a veteran. He went through the same stuff I did, and he still served the country." Pap was very keen on second chances, he often spoke of the many opportunities he was given throughout his life and how his previous experiences shaped him. He always told me "Everyone deserves second chances because everyone makes mistakes."

"No one word can describe your Pap, he was the best man I knew... He never met a stranger" - April Prather.

Another memory that will always stick with me was when Pap and my Grandma, "Mimi", took me to my first MLB game. Like everyone else in my family, Pap loved the Cincinnati Reds. I loved his stories of The Big Red Machine teams in the 70's. His favorite player was Pete Rose, and he loved Rose so much that he adopted the nickname "Pete" (His real name was Lee Roy). I was around 8-9 when they took me to Cincinnati, this was right around the time the Reds built a Pete Rose statue outside of their ballpark, and Pap was excited to see it. The statue is huge, it depicts Rose sliding hard, head-first into a base, an iconic move that earned him the nickname "Charlie Hustle". Pap and Mimi went above and beyond with this trip, we took a tour of the stadium, learning its history. After the tour, Pap took me to the site of Pete Rose's record-breaking hit #4,192 on the ground of Riverfront Stadium, the former home of the Reds. He could easily recall when Rose broke the record, "I reckon I was watching it on TV, I'm sure your daddy was there too". After the tour, we watched the Reds match up against the Washington Nationals, I don't remember who won but I do remember Devin Mesaraco, the Reds catcher at the time, hitting a 400 ft home run to left to give the Reds a lead in the first inning. Pap turned to me as the ball landed and said, "Won't be long and you'll be doing that". Although I haven't hit any 400ft homers recently, every time I step on a baseball field, I remember the games he came to watch me play, and I know he's watching now too. I play every game for him.

One of the final times I spoke to Pap, he had been moved into a nursing home in La Grange. He had cancer, we knew he probably didn't have much longer, and we tried to see him every day. I asked Pap about his time in the Navy, I had heard bits and pieces of his service throughout my life, but I had never asked outright about his experiences. "What was your favorite part about the Navy Pap?" I asked, his voice broke very often now, and he never talked with the same conviction he once did, but he was still a great storyteller, "Probably boot camp, we were always doing something y'know? Once I got out of boot camp, we kinda just hung around, but I got to see places I probably never would have seen, met some great people, and had a great time y'know?" After he finished, and moved on to another of his many stories, I couldn't help but wonder, "Boot camp? Really?". But as I thought about Pap, I realized that for as long as I had known him, he always loved the simple things. To him making friends was simple, so he was friends with everyone; He had been playing and watching baseball for so long that it was simple for him so he shared his love of the game with everyone. Boot camp was just another opportunity to be social for him, and he loved it.

"There has never been a better man than your Pap, he always treated everyone so well. He made sure everyone felt included and loved" - April Prather

Pap passed away in December 2020, a combination of his cancer and Covid-19. I know he's watching me as I'm writing this, and I know he wouldn't have wanted all of the crying and boohooing I've done over him. I know he didn't want to spend the last part of his life in the nursing home, although the "pretty nurses" as he put it, might have made up for it a little. There's only one thing I never understood about him, how he always stayed on top of the world. Despite growing up poor with a dozen siblings, despite losing his daughter Leah a couple of years before he passed himself, and despite spending his final months stuck in a nursing home; His love and great attitude never wavered. As I've grown up, I have often struggled to control my emotions, and although I have many positive figures in my life, there is no one that I will look up to more than Pap, and I am so very grateful to have been his family.

PURPLE MONKEY

GEORGIA SNIDER

Christy Ann Martine once said, "Create a safe place within yourself that no one will ever find, somewhere the madness of this world can never touch."

When things got rough I always had my Purple Monkey. Purple Monkey was my safe place. From an early age, I learned that safe spaces don't have to be houses or locations but can be objects so I clung to a stuffed animal. Having a rough home life meant many ups and downs, but Purple Monkey never left my side. It was us against the world. Purple Monkey was, well, purple and had long arms and legs which were my favorite feature. He also had "princess" written in bright pink font across his belly. He had little black sewn-on eyes and a big thin smile that you could usually find thread hanging from. You could certainly tell Purple Monkey was well-loved because of the worn spots on his limbs and the ear you could visibly see was sewn back on.

Purple Monkey was always smiling mostly because he didn't have a choice but he was a very comforting companion. As a child, I was always timid but Purple Monkey was always there for me to hold onto. When I would leave the house or have to talk to people Purple Monkey had to be there. I would always nervously rub his arms and legs but he didn't seem to mind. He was always understanding. Whenever I would be upset or have my world flipped upside down those little eyes and his big smile would listen when I couldn't go to anyone else. He was a great listener and shoulder to cry on.

"Never fear to deliberately walk through dark places, for that is how you reach the light on the other side." - Vernon Howard.

I can't remember receiving Purple Monkey as a gift but I remember the challenges it brought when I needed to go out in public. One weekend I had to leave Purple Monkey in the car when we were going in to eat at IHOP. Usually, when we went on outings I would hide behind my parents and cry when people approached me but this time things were different. We arrived at the restaurant and I was with my dad's parents whom I call Nana and Paw Paw. After we sat down at the table and waited it came time to order which is where things took a turn. The sweet woman waiting on our table tried to simply ask me what I wanted to eat as a sweet interaction that you usually see people having with younger children. However, I did not take to that well. I had an absolute conniption. I started screaming at the woman and of course, I couldn't talk yet so it was nothing but tears and erratic words. All I remember after having my fit was the relief I experienced when they went out to the car and retrieved Purple Monkey for me. I was spoiled but I couldn't help it, I needed my companion to be in the restaurant with me. He was always there for me so I felt it was unfair to just leave him alone in the car.

"Sewing is the thread that stitches memories together."- Unknown

As I had mentioned earlier, you could tell that Purple Monkey was well-loved. One of the many things that had to be repaired was his ear. I had rubbed it right off. I vividly remember this happening because once again, I had a conniption over it.

"Don't put that needle in Purple Monkey, you're going to hurt him!" I cried.

My Nana reassured me by saying, "It'll be just like taking a trip to the doctor's office. It'll take every bit of ten minutes and he'll be good as new."

At the time I thought she was insane for wanting to hurt my Purple Monkey but I agreed for him to have the procedure so he didn't have to walk around with a missing ear. If I had to keep both of my ears Purple Monkey had to keep both of his. I was extremely distraught over this for days because you could see that the stitching was a different color purple but I learned that made him unique from any of the other Purple Monkeys out there. Mine was special and had his little mark because of me. I had loved him to pieces... literally.

"All good things must come to an end. That's why they're called good things– otherwise they're just ... ordinary." - Joyce Rachelle

One of the moments in my life that crushed me was when I moved in the seventh grade. During the process of moving, I was packing up stuffed animals and deciding which ones to keep with me and which to get rid of. At the time I was in middle school so I saw myself as being cool which meant not thinking about stuffed animals. However, all of this changed when I was going through the last of my belongings in my closet and discovered Purple Monkey was not there. I went through all of the bags and boxes again and checked all of the parts of my loft bed thinking he may have been stored in one of the drawers but Purple Monkey was gone. There was no way of getting him back. I had found old school supplies, clothes, holiday cards, and even random baby teeth but no sign of Purple Monkey. My parents even helped me look for days because they knew how important he was to me. I've moved and still occasionally look through the basement for Purple Monkey trying to fulfill the hope that he was misplaced and will one day show up.

I don't know where he is now but I occasionally think that maybe losing Purple Monkey was a good thing. If I still had an attachment to him I don't know how I would act socially or if I would have any friends at all. I was petrified to associate with people when I had him but had to learn how to do things on my own. His loss taught me that it's okay to move out of your comfort zone. I do miss my Purple Monkey with every part of my being but since branching out I have been in theatrical productions, given speeches, had leadership roles, and led teams. We all have things in our lives that shape us into the people we are whether they stay with us or get lost along the way. Purple Monkey was what pushed me into being the person I am and what I will become. I will never forget or regret what that sweet little monkey did for me.

TOBACCO LIFE

COLBY STIVERS

I woke up to my ceiling lights blaring in my eyes. My dad got me up to help strip tobacco, I thought. I went back to sleep. He returned to my room to wake me up, but this time, In a calm voice that you just cannot get mad at, he said, "Hey, wake up." Sometimes, after my dad talked to me about helping the night before, I woke up the next morning, relieved he forgot to wake me up. But deep down, I knew he had taken one look at me while I was fast asleep and gave me grace. That is something he did not experience. His family, for generations, lived off of getting up early, and working hard all day long, coming home to a delicious cooked meal prepared by the also, hard-working wife, and then off to bed. They would repeat this for many years. It is a very rough lifestyle, but they were used to it. Those were real men. Don't get me started about the lack of masculinity and toughness in men today. I wouldn't say this 8 years ago, but I am truly grateful I got a taste of what everyday life was like for a countryman.

As I wearily got out of my warm bed, I was thrilled to see Dad had made me a delicious breakfast. Every morning before school he did this, up until he started his job as a bus driver. I do miss those days. Our farm is around 150 acres, not including my grandpa's 250 and Kevin Flood's 150. We all work for each other and help one another out. This farm holds many fields growing varieties of hay, corn, wheat, and many years of tobacco. And cattle have always been worked. This may have been the looks of the traditional farm.

As I entered the stripping room, I was engulfed by the warmth of the coal-burning steamer and the dusty, stuffy air. The room is about twenty by ten feet in dimension with a long wooden counter for the tobacco to lay on the right. To the left is the furnace and the tobacco baler. One time I banged my mouth against the metal baler and chipped a tooth, and I never went to the dentist.

I then sleepily and sullenly walked to my usual spot not knowing how much I would yearn for and cling to the laughs and memories in this small room. Specifically, the ones where we roast Henry County and Eminence sports. Not to mention, Kevin Flood is a basketball ref. Let's just say, he makes some questionable calls every once in a while. You may want to know that Kevin does live in a run-down farmhouse that has seen better days, but for some reason, when you see him in public, he displays all the style in the way he dresses. He's a very unique fellow. While stripping tobacco one day, I told him I was going to have dinner at his house. He responded by saying, "Welp, hope you like coon!" then followed with a loud laugh. I love his laugh. To this day, I still am not sure if he was serious about that response.

I also learned not to say "stripping" in the public. In elementary school, I asked my sister if we were going to strip (forgetting to say tobacco) today a little too loudly, and I got some looks. With all that said, a day in the stripping room, no matter how boring it could get doing the same thing over again is a day I can't forget, especially the times everyone would share unfortunate bathroom experiences. But you get the point. I loved striping.

Every year, tobacco fields attract the Tobacco Worm. Here I am, just walking down a row in the tobacco field picking up sticks, and the next thing I know, I've been hit. Green and chunky juices absorbed into my shirt. What went from all business and hard work, turned into a worm battle. Most of them were tiny but some were fat and juicy. Usually we would get in trouble for stopping our work, but we didn't care. The whole time, everyone would be looking down for the next tobacco worm to launch.

The process of raising tobacco goes from planting, to moisturizing, to conditioning, to cutting, and to drying. Then it is stripped from their stalks and pressed in a tobacco bale and shipped off to sell. The bales weigh around 700 pounds each. Before the drying process can occur, the already cut tobacco needs to be loaded on to wagons and taken to barns to be housed.

You know those times when you've laughed so much and so hard that breathing becomes difficult and you feel weak? Well, this happens almost every time when we house tobacco. Housing, if you don't know, is a very physically demanding and tiring job. I stand on the wagon, while my father and uncle are up in the tiers of the barn racking the tobacco, with me handing tobacco up to them. This can be especially strenuous when the tobacco is wet, which becomes very heavy. Anyways, around three years ago, my cousin was housing tobacco with us and his dad told him to get the tractor and bring up some more wagons of tobacco. He left. For some reason we didn't have much belief in him to do this, so they went on rambling about this until my uncle said, "Watch him bring back the salvage wagon." We got a big laugh out of this. My dad said, "Come back with no wagon!" Immediately my uncle bursts into his iconic laugh that I also love. At this point, I am at the brink of tears because I'm laughing so hard, and like I mentioned before, lifting this tobacco was pretty much impossible at the moment. The funny thing was, it wasn't for another twenty minutes before my cousin came back. This may not be as funny on paper as it was in person, but it's a moment I cherish.

Getting sick from Tobacco was something we would absolutely dread, but not surprised when we got it. I got it twice. It was our last year we raised tobacco when I got nic sick (or green tobacco sickness). The tough part was, on that day we worked in tobacco, I had invited a friend to help. And–he got sick also. I felt so guilty and responsible for this happening, especially since I knew his mom told him she didn't want him getting sick. My experience with nic sick goes like this: I get home from housing tobacco for several hours feeling just sore. Eventually, I would get a suspicious rush of sleepiness. A few minutes afterwards I get hit with a gut wrenching sting in my head, which then makes way for the sweat. Then I'm met with nausea. The next thing I know, I'm lying flat on my back in the bathroom breathing quickly in and slowly out, waiting to throw up. But the worst thing was, I could not vomit for the life of me. I'm sweating–I'm dizzy–I'm nauseous and I can't let it all out. Thankfully, getting this type of sickness doesn't last long. The next morning I was feeling quite fine. But, that doesn't take away how miserable I felt that night.

When most people hear the word tobacco they think nicotine, addiction, unhealthy, bad. But when I hear the word tobacco, my thoughts are racing with the happy, uniting, arduous, hilarious, and valuable time spent with family and friends. Unfortunately, that time spent is to support a terrible cause in smoking. But I've never been so thankful for the family God put me in. I can't imagine what situation could be better. My father and his family taught me toughness, and living life without complaint, while my mother, and her family taught me the greatest love of all time. The love of Jesus. Put those two together and you have a man of

God. I mentioned the sicknesses and hard work that I dreaded because I wanted to make something clear. That all the tiring and miserable times do not compare to the joy that I cling to. God has given me these memories, lessons and experiences to shape me into the man that I must be. The suffering creates endurance in me. And the times I experience goodness and greatness gives me something to hold on to. Through this, I know that in darkness, there is *always* light.

MY DAD

KAIDEN WILSON

Most children's first love is their mother; mine, however, was the tall guy who shadowed over me. Dad was my hero, the one I looked up to and worked tirelessly to impress. I credit the young man I am today to the towering figure I called Daddy.

There was passion and strength in his hands and his eyes, and I remember that still today. He was a very tall man with a bright smile and everyone knew him by his smile. He had a muscular build and short black hair. Most people knew him because of the tattoos on his arm and his dark skin tone. My dad was very kind to everyone. He helped anyone who needed help, treated everyone with respect, and would give you the shirt off of his back or the money in his pocket if you needed it.

He never expected anything in return because he did it out of the kindness of his heart. You could do wrong by him, and he would still help you if you asked. He cared more about his word than anything. He wouldn't tell you that he was going to do something, and then not do it. He would make sure he did everything that he could at 100%.

Every little kid remembers their first core memory with their father. When I was eight years old, I was in the car with my dad and we were doing donuts in his old 2012 Mustang GT 5.0. Next, we took off after he was done with the donuts and went super fast. Now, I think this is the whole reason I love going fast. It reminds me of my dad because it's something I always do because of the trust I had in Dad. It never scared me. I always felt safe with my dad, even with him driving as fast as he did. Dad always said, "You will be able to catch as many fish and be a better fisherman than me one day."

A few years later I started to learn how to fish because I wanted to do more things with my dad. We made a bet about who was going to catch more and we started at the same time. He caught the first few fish, then I started to catch them back to back and he started to catch more. It got me down because I didn't want to lose to him, I just wanted to make him proud. Then out of nowhere, I caught the biggest fish I've ever caught. It was an eight-pound bass! Then my dad came over and said to me, "That was the size of the biggest fish I've ever caught, too!" He said he was very proud of me.

He said that he was done, that I had beaten him, and maybe I'm already starting to get better than him.

March 14th, 2022 was the last time I talked to my dad before he died. I was talking to my Dad about baseball and how I had a game coming up. I was wondering if he was going to be able to come to the game because I didn't know if he was working. When he said he was going to be able to, I smiled really big to show how happy I was about it. We started to joke around about something mom did, and then I told him that I was about to go to bed. I said goodnight, I love you, and he said it back.

Then the worst day of my life happened. March 15th, 2022 my dad died and it ruined my world because I lost something irreplaceable, my father. Everyone knows how to live with their parents around, but nobody is prepared to learn how to live without their parents. At a young age, you don't understand as much until you are older. Losing the parent who was there for guidance at 14 years old is one of the hardest things because it's such a hard change to everything.

At a young age, you want to question why they were taken from you, but it will never be answered by somebody because nobody truly knows the answer. My dad is the reason I do everything with 100%; I try to make him proud even if he isn't with me physically. I want to make sure that I still can make his name proud and let people know that my dad raised a good man, and it's always been hard since he died because I'm going along as life goes. After all, I can't ask him for guidance, and I'm still learning a lot. I wrote this memoir because the memories are something that I cherish. It has been 631 days since he died but his memories will stay alive through me.

www.ingramcontent.com/pod-product-compliance
Lightning Source LLC
Chambersburg PA
CBHW072227190626
46809CB00017B/1056

* 9 7 8 1 9 5 8 4 1 4 3 7 8 *